I0640961

Firebrand Firestorm

The Ancestors of Bjorn Esterday

Volume 05

Anticipation

March & April 1776

Wynter Sommers

USA Copyright © 2015 GJ dePillis
© 2015, TXu001966602 / 2015-05-08 and TXu001983965 / 2015-11-04

Library of Congress Control Number: 2020943167

Published by Pure Force Enterprises, Inc.
California, USA
Since 2002

INGRAM

INGRAM® Distribution

ISBN-13: 978-1-7184-0017-7
ISBN-10: 1-7184-0017-9

DEDICATION

To those who feel strongly about truth,
justice, and the integrity of America;
your honorable actions make us proud.
To those who wonder if their daily
choices matter; your small decisions
impact generations to come.
To those everyday people who don't think
they have what it takes; when you strive
for extraordinary things, the impossible
becomes reality.
Your dreams today become our future
tomorrow.
Thank you for everything you do.

Bjorn Esterday
Was Not Born Yesterday
Series

Firebrand (15 Volumes+Conversation Station Book)
Edges (9 Stories +Conversation Station Book)
Gone (18 Stories + Conversation Station Book)

Bjorn EDGES Series

EDGES Book 1-Swift Encounter
EDGES Book 2-Rousing Attack
EDGES Book 3-One Foot Under
EDGES Book 4-Earthshake
EDGES Book 5-Broken String
EDGES Book 6-Key Witness
EDGES Book 7-Who is She?
EDGES Book 8-Vanish
EDGES Book 9-Chase or Die

Bjorn Series Alternate Reading Plan

1st	Edges Book 1		22nd	Gone Book 10
2nd	Edges Book 2		23rd	Firebrand Vol 9
3rd	Gone Book 1		24rd	Gone Book 11
4th	Firebrand Vol 1		25th	Firebrand Vol 10
5th	Edges Book 3		26th	Gone Book 12
6th	Firebrand Vol 2		27th	Gone Book 13
7th	Gone Book 2		28th	Firebrand Vol 11
8th	Gone Book 3		29th	Gone Book 14
9th	Firebrand Vol 3		30th	Firebrand Vol 12
10th	Gone Book 4		31st	Gone Book 15
11th	Firebrand Vol 4		32nd	Firebrand Vol 13
12th	Gone Book 5		33rd	Gone Book 16
13th	Gone Book 6		34th	Firebrand Vol 14
14th	Edges Book 4		35th	Gone Book 17
15th	Firebrand Vol 5		36th	Firebrand Vol15 (End)
16th	Gone Book 7		37th	Gone Book 18 (End)
17th	Firebrand Vol 6		38th	Edges Book 5
18th	Gone Book 8		39th	Edges Book 6
19th	Firebrand Vol 7		40th	Edges Book 7
20th	Gone Book 9		41st	Edges Book 8
21st	Firebrand Vol 8		42nd	Edges Book 9(End)

Acknowledgement

We acknowledge those who actively build peace. We acknowledge all the selfless talent which contributed to creating meaningful tokens of consideration and sharing. We acknowledge that every person has a daily choice of right or wrong... and we thank you for choosing the right, good, honorable path filled with integrity because that is the difficult and brave path. Small choices today become lasting monuments of loving hope tomorrow

CONTENTS

0 PREFACE

After Jane had situated Polly in the Dunlap home by using the boar meat as lodging payment, Jane pursued justice to uncover her Uncle's past relations, which may have led to his demise. Meanwhile Bryce Aiden Tyler, Uncle Floyd's former business partner, is conducting his own experiments.

Will their paths converge or diverge?

Will truth be found and is the effort expended for truth worth the personal cost to Jane?

What impact could the efforts of an unknown woman have, especially one who now has no social standing in these new Colonies?

Would it not be easier for Jane to

accept the fact that she will be even more destitute than she had imagined? Will Jane still be able to help her staff get new jobs and also be able to seek employment herself, accepting yet a new lower station in life? Why should she fight to maintain what was her uncle's?

What drives Polly to hope and continue to dream that this inhospitable New World is the place she should be? Why does Polly hope her husband is still alive? Why does she not simply accept what is easy and abandon her past?

When should we ourselves accept negative circumstances and when should we push against the odds to continue to pursue a dream, a goal, or objective justice, honor and truth? What ethics drive us?.

1 CHAPTER 35: (APRIL 1776) Polly and Jane continue to chat

Jane gazed out the window of the carriage. They were passing trees and wild grasses. She adjusted her skirts as her legs were getting tingly from sitting in the same position. As Jane looked out the window she tried to see the driver. From her vantage point, she could not see anything other than the horses galloping along.

She turned to Polly and smiled.

Polly smiled back. She commented softly, "Your kindness rescued me and my unborn from certain death. Thank you."

Jane simply shook her head as if to indicate no thanks was needed, and said, "I'm sure you'd do the same for me if our situations were reversed."

"You being from England and me from Ireland... If I only knew that, I don't think I would, Jane." "I see." Jane smiled politely.

"But seeing your manner is so contrary to the English I have encountered, and seeing how Silversmith puts her faith in you... After getting to know you, I would say if our situations were reversed, I would surely render aid as you have rendered to me today."

"Thank you, Polly. Quite an endorsement. I'm sure we shall be grand friends." Jane smiled politely and looked out the window.

There was a pause. A silent pause. A long pause.

Polly took a deep breath and asked, "So, face powder... Can you get the sort you need over here in the colonies? The type you got back in Europe?"

"No, actually," Jane explained, pleased Polly decided to leave her vitriol behind. "I have not had time to explore all the boutiques here, but I do not think one can easily get what one is used to in London. What I can purchase is powdered clay or Bentonite."

"Bentonite?" Polly asked. "You mean what the furniture makers use to fill hallow legs to make the chair feel heavier and more sturdy?"

"Oh, no. That must be something else," Jane dismissed. "Bentonite is what *Pliny the Elder* and even Cleopatra had used to tighten the skin. When mixed with vinegar, it makes a foamy poultice clay for the face, which deep cleans it once it dries until it cracks on your face. If you use just the dry powder, it will keep your face from shine all day."

"Isn't Bentonite green?" Polly asked.

"Well," Jane thought, "It does have a foggy-green-cast to it, but the color counteracts the ruddy tones in my face and the powder keeps my skin from being shiny. My skin was always shiny with the lead based *blancs*."

"So you found a face powder you like over here?" Polly asked glad to speak of something inconsequential.

"But, I simply cannot relinquish the use of lip paint," Jane explained. "If I have to find cherries, or pomegranate seeds to stain my lips, I shall. I have heard of some who will scrape the white cochineal bugs from a cactus pad in the hotter climates and dry them, then grind them to use for the deep red color and mix with a touch of oil to apply to one's lips."

"Do you do that? Make your own?" Polly asked.

Jane held up her hand in protest, "Oh, no. I purchase. I don't make. All I know is that when one has a bad day, a bit of red stain on one's lips makes one feel as if one is in the French Courts, you see."

Polly commented, "I suppose cosmetic paints might have a different meaning in this country."

"Last I checked," Jane started with a smile, "...we don't have any Queens nor Kings on this island to cause a silly fuss about which cosmetics and perfumes we can and cannot wear. We are all too busy trying to survive, you see"

"Yes. I can live without a ruling family quite easily," Polly surmised. "I learned a couple of languages as a child, so I've seen the impact kings and queens have on people of different cultures."

"Different languages?" Jane asked.

"English, German, French, and some Italian, and a touch of Latin," Polly replied.

"To have studied all those languages, you must also have fine penmanship,"

Jane observed

"I believe I do," Polly replied.

"A shame your talents were wasted as a housemaid. I shall look for opportunities to give to Silversmith to expand her talents. A challenge makes one grow, don't you think? I do hope Silversmith does not feel trapped in her current position..." Jane sat up straight suddenly and continued, "I've made up my mind, Polly. You have inspired me. I shall look for ways to challenge Silversmith..." Jane smiled brightly.

"I'm glad. I may not know Silversmith personally, but I do know the Irish spirit is strong and ready for a challenge," Polly observed.

Jane extracted a bore-bristle hairbrush, looked at it, observing, "I know pig's hair was stiff enough to make a good brush, but I never really thought much about how one may taste. Boiled, roasted or fried..." She smiled at Polly, "You've given me a different perspective on several things I had not given much thought to."

Polly replied, "And you are helping me to find lodgings so maybe I can find out if my husband lives or has been scalped or enslaved..."

"I think you are presentable enough to convince the Dunlap printers to take you in. You'll have to write to me and tell me how you fare," Jane smiled.

"Write to you?" Polly asked. "So, you won't be staying in the area? You won't visit me when the baby arrives, then?"

"I know it looks as if I've packed for an extended venture, but I'll only be staying a few days. Then I return home to determine where Silversmith and I shall live next..." Jane trailed off. "I always prepare for the absolute worst case...but I'd like to make sure you are situated properly. As a friend, that is. It's only fitting. We can write to each other."

Polly took a deep breath as she stared out the window. "I don't think I can ever go back to our log home. Button and I had a dream of building twenty or thirty homes... owning hundreds of acres.... That's now a shattered dream...." Polly trailed off.

"Nonsense," Jane encouraged. "Just modify your dream to build twenty-nine... Thirty is far too ostentatious, but twenty-nine is a more ladylike goal... even if you must collect the materials and build them all by yourselves, focus on that goal."

"I'd have to dress in trousers, get the papers of ownership, and then dress like a man when I obtain supplies..." Polly chortled at the absurd image of herself in trousers.

"Then you must dress in trousers to get your home building supplies and wear lip rouge to have fun... maybe even wear them both at the same time." Jane smiled, "If building is your dream... do it. Don't allow circumstances to stop you from achieving...there will always be something to blame until you decide to stop blaming and take that purposeful step toward your future."

"Future?" Polly shook her head as if she pictured a rather bleak tomorrow.

Jane continued, "Yes, a future of hard work, but also of great rewards reaped by your future generations," Jane smiled at Polly's belly, then back up to Polly's face. Jane clearly stated, "Now, back to concentrating on today. Let us see if the Dunlaps enjoy Silversmith's unusual concept of fried pig belly for a morning snack..."

"And what if these Dunlaps don't take me in, Jane? What if wild boar meat or this fried Bacoun... is not accepted as my lodging fee?" Polly asked.

2 CHAPTER 36: (MARCH 1776) Silversmith at the Wilson Mansion

Silversmith stumbled under the weight of the bags. She squeezed through the servants entrance. The kitchen was crowded with staff.

"Is this area called Rising Sun?" Silversmith asked a woman who looked harried and rushed.

That woman, one of Lady Sarah Wilson's housekeepers, beckoned Silversmith to follow in order to show Silversmith to Jane Hargreaves' room. There Silversmith dropped off some of the bags.

"Yes," the housekeeper replied.

Silversmith asked, "If I must run errands, are there shops nearby this estate?"

"No," the housekeeper answered. "Summer Hill is small, but remote."

"Am I in Summer Hill or Rising Sun?" Silversmith asked confused.

The housekeeper paused, "William Penn and his Quakers settled the area in 1702, calling it Summer Hill. In 1720, Henry Reynolds built a tavern and coach stop. He had a sign with a picture of a sun rising over the horizon, so some call this place Rising Sun."

"Coach?" Silversmith asked, "As in horses for hire?"

"You and your mistress may wish to know Nottingham Lot seventeen is the only place to hire a horse if you need to run errands."

"How far is it from here? A walk?" Silversmith asked, "How far do the horses go?".

The housekeeper thought, "Nottingham Lot seventeen is a long and healthy walk from here, but their hired horses will take you anywhere you wish. "

Then, after most of the luggage was deposited in the room where Jane would stay, Silversmith was left with just one simple bag. The housekeeper took Silversmith upstairs to where she would be staying. She was instructed on the proper staircase to ascend and descend to attend to her mistress' needs.

The housekeeper explained, "Each of the master rooms has several hooks which trigger a bell in each one of the servants quarters. So, each guest room has two pull cords. One for the main servants hall and one, to use at night, to a specific servant. The room where your employer will stay is connected to the room upstairs where you will stay."

"So only I will be awakened by my employer?" Silversmith asked.

"Correct," said the housekeeper as she pointed to a bell in the corner of the room where Silversmith was to sleep. The room was the size of a large closet. The bed was small and narrow, pushed up against the wall. The only furnishings were one table with one drawer, a single candle in its candle stick, and a chamber pot in the far corner.

The housekeeper continued, "And we don't rename you after your master's name, so you will always be named your name. Since the guests invited have been asked to remain for the season, we placed a wooden plank on your door and there is a paint brush and can there. Select a symbol and that is how you will be known." The housekeeper pointed to some of the other rooms painted with a small square, circle, etc..

"Could I simply write my name?" Silversmith asked.

The housekeeper stopped and gave a single sharp laugh. "You write?" Then when Silversmith didn't respond in kind, the housekeeper added, "You can do what you like. Just remember if you do write, not everybody reads. We need to know what room you'll be in. You may leave suddenly or stay the whole of summer. We don't know..."

The housekeeper walked along the hall and opened a cupboard. "Linens, here," she said.

"Oh, that's very forward thinking," Silversmith commented, trying to put Lady Sarah Wilson's housekeeper at ease.

The housekeeper handed Silversmith some folded sheets for her to make up her own bed. "I'll leave you to unpack then." The housekeeper started for the door.

Silversmith hurried after her, with folded sheets still in hand. "Ma'am, I've been asked to run an errand. So, I won't have time to unpack now as I must leave immediately." Silversmith ran back to her room, and dropped her bag on the mattress along with the folded sheets. The housekeeper was already walking away. Silversmith hurried after her down the hallway.

As Silversmith bustled after the housekeeper, she said, "I would so appreciate any insight on the background of the other guests, if you could share that," Silversmith urged.

"You've never been here, then. I don't recall you," The housekeeper grunted. "No Ma'am. This is my first time at the estate," Silversmith commented.

"The basics, then. Follow me as I've plenty to do. The lady of the house is Miss Sarah Wilson... from Carolina society." The housekeeper hurried off assuming Silversmith was keeping up.

"I've not been to the Colony of Carolina," Silversmith responded.

The housekeeper shared, "I've been

with Sarah Wilson since she arrived in this country... well since she ran away and gained position in society."

"Ran away?" Silversmith commented.

"Lady Sarah Wilson, that's your hostess' name, is very open about her history," the housekeeper started. "She says that prevents blackmailers from trying to elicit money from her, so she's quite public about her background."

"Background?" Silversmith echoed.

The housekeeper bustled past the other staff, speaking as she headed back downstairs, "Sarah Wilson, part of Queen Charlotte's court, eloped in 1771 with a diamond necklace...not a man. She was caught and shipped to the American colonies to be sold as a slave here, but she ran away right after she was purchased. She changed her name to Marchioness de Waldegrave, Sister of the Queen. After all she had stolen a couple of trinkets from Queen Charlotte that would make her story believable.

She consorted with Carolina society for over a year. Those society doors opened along with their purses always fawning to impress the queen's sister."

"But if she wasn't the queen's sister, wasn't her story a lie?" Silversmith asked.

"That was her income. She was a confidence trickster. It was her occupation. But she always paid her loyal staff, so who am I to judge where her money comes from as long as I get paid?" The housekeeper shrugged as she burst through the busy kitchen where the staff was already chopping and slicing.

The housekeeper continued, "Eventually, the truth caught up with *Marchioness de Waldegrave,* and she changed her name back to Sarah Wilson and acquired this estate, promising never to return to either Carolina colony. In today's modern times of 1776 she spends her days entertaining in hopes of finding a legitimate heir of some sort to marry."

"I see," said Silversmith astonished. "She was never arrested?"

"Indeed not. They couldn't find enough evidence, so she has no record. She was savvy enough to have befriended influential authorities of the area so they took pity on her and simply asked her to leave, which we were already preparing to do. It doesn't matter to me. A house needs running no matter where it is."

"So how should I address the mistress of this estate? Lady Sarah Wilson? Marchioness de Waldegrave? or Miss Sarah? "

"If you want to be on her good side, I'd pick either Lady or Duchess Wilson. She thinks if you say a title frequently enough, it'll stick. This home is called the Wilson estate. It's not named something memorable like... Evenfalls. The lands are slight. We only have this structure and the stable out back with a space for the stable boys to sleep in."

"So, she collected enough money to

purchase it?" Silversmith prodded.

"Well, no. She's has numerous paramours whose gifts provided for this estate. She doesn't own this land, but you must always act as if she does or she'll throw you out. Her ladyship has no tolerance for people who attempt to demean her standing in society."

"Noted. Thank you. Where is the owner of this estate?" Silversmith asked. "The owner is in Europe," the housekeeper shrugged.

"Ah," Silversmith said, "And what of the other guests? Are they of society? I don't want to offend them, you see... this being my first time here... at the Wilson Estate?"

"Those invited or those who will actually come? Let's see... There is Abigail Stoneman... Owner of the Merchant's Coffee House and Tea House... and she's talking about opening up a ballroom in Newport... she was invited."

"Didn't she have a coffee house in Boston... at the site of the March 1770 Massacre?"

"She did, but her family perseveres. Let's see... another Bostonian is arriving, Elizabeth Hager. She re- shoes horses."

"Blacksmith Handy Betty?"

"That's the one. She's bringing her friend from Maryland, Jane Burgess, also a blacksmith, now widow blacksmith as of 1773. She runs her husband's business now," the housekeeper replied.

"So the guest list is not actual society, but rather trades folk? Blacksmiths?" Silversmith prodded.

The housekeeper nodded, "I think the Butterworth twins will be coming, but their mother won't, rest her soul. Mary Butterworth was nearly 90 when she died last year. It was a February funeral. Lady Wilson was most upset, but she still plans to invite the twin boys, in their

40's now...Lady Sarah Wilson doesn't want to chance being lonely, you see..."

"Is the Butterworth family in a trade, as well?" Silversmith asked.

"Of sorts," the housekeeper explained, "Mary Butterworth was a Puritan housewife. Died in February last year, 1775. Nearly 90, she was. She became wealthy from counterfeiting over 1,000 pounds of currency and teaching others to join her enterprise. Never got convicted. "

"Never?" Silversmith asked.

The housekeeper shrugged, "She came from a prominent family, so the townsfolk looked the other way. She may have spent a few days in jail, but never formally convicted."

"So just her family name kept her from prison?" Silversmith asked.

"How did they put it...?" The housekeeper thought a moment as she recollected,   "Hmm...vehemently suspected to be guilty of making counterfeiting and uttering the bills of public credit in New England, particularly the Bills of his Majesty's Province of Massachusetts Bay and the Colony of Road Island, I think it was...Lady Sarah Wilson respected Mary Butterworth. She was inventive."

"Inventive? With copying pound notes?" Silversmith asked.

"She was a housekeeping artist," The housekeeper explained with a smile of admiration, "She would take starched cotton cloth, iron a genuine bill to lift the ink, then iron that onto a blank paper and touch up the artwork with her quill pen. She'd sell her bills off at half the face value of the bill. "

"So, does Lady Sarah Wilson prefer to invite mostly women to her soirées?" Silversmith asked.

All the kitchen staff were busy organizing provisions in anticipation of several guests arriving all at once.

"Well, the men are all business sorts," The housekeeper explained, "When they decide to make an appearance... I don't know how they make money, but they always seem to have plenty of it. They are frequent guests, here. But the women – the learned ones- all seem to be friends of Benjamin Franklin, and for some reason Lady Wilson keeps inviting them and they politely decline, then get together to meet in that town about one day's carriage ride away."

"Why do they meet there instead of coming here?" Silversmith asked as she stepped out of the way of the pantry being restocked with dry goods from other members of the household.

"I don't rightly know," the housekeeper shared. "Maybe they prefer catching a glimpse of Benjamin Franklin instead of having a proper meal, here. I don't rightly care, neither. Fewer guests means less work for me..." The housekeeper replied.

"Agreed," Silversmith said. "So, does Lady Wilson have friends from the Carolina Colonies?"

The housekeeper paused as she handed Silversmith some sacks of flour to hold while she reached behind them in the pantry to get a spare iron. "Lady Wilson may have met the Timothy family when she was in South Carolina. Peter Timothy had a sweetheart and I think Sarah Wilson wanted to seduce the man away."

"Seduce?" Silversmith repeated.

"Well, that Peter Timothy's mother, Elizabeth Timothy, was a widow who ran the South Carolina Gazette. Smart business woman. She knew how to make money and Lady Sarah Wilson was always friendly to those who could supply her with money."

The housekeeper sniffed as she walked to the hearth, stoked the fire, then placed the iron on the hot embers. She looked at a stack of washed, wrinkled cloth napkins.

"Tell me more about Elizabeth Timothy," Silversmith prodded.

The housekeeper accidentally knocked over a portion of the linen napkins. She retrieved some of the napkins from the floor, and then walked to the table to fold them.

"I'd have one of the girls do this folding, but they are all scrambling to prepare the house for guests, you see..." the Housekeeper commented.

The housekeeper folded a napkin, and picked up the next one, glancing at the iron in the hearth to see if it was hot enough. "Elizabeth Timothy was with child when her husband Lewis Timothy died back in 1739. Fell off a horse, I think. She printed an announcement that even though she's expecting her seventh child, she'd still run the paper. So her son, Peter, would be nearly 40 years old by today."

"And how did the South Carolina Gazette fare being run by a mother of seven children?" Silversmith asked.

"The business prospered," the housekeeper replied glancing at the fireplace to see if the iron was yet hot. She continued, "Even started to sell pocket Bibles and other books about courtship and marriage around 1746."

"So, does this Elizabeth or Peter Timothy, do they meet in town with the ambassador Benjamin Franklin or do they come here to the estate?" Silversmith asked.

"The Timothy family has never been here," the housekeeper stated. "I'd say they might meet with Mr. Franklin if he were passing through the Meeting Town. They say that Mr. Franklin invested in Mrs.Timothy's South Carolina Gazette. Supposedly, her Dutch work ethic coupled with Mr. Benjamin Franklin's investment gold, helped the widow Timothy be the first woman newspaperman in South Carolina. So, it is natural to assume that Mr. Franklin would welcome any of the Timothy family when Mr. Franklin is in Meeting town."

"Meeting town?" Silversmith asked.

"Well, Meeting Town is the local name for it. It is a full day's carriage ride away. That's where the respectable folk go and meet. Timothy, Wright, and..."

"Wright?" Silversmith asked.

"Susanna Wright. She is acquainted with Mr. Franklin, as well... Don't tell me you've never heard of Susanna Wright!"

"I don't think I have," Silversmith confessed.

"I dare say..." The housekeeper shook her head. She strode to the hearth and licked her finger, then tapped the handle of the iron. Now satisfied it was hot enough, she grabbed a dry rag, wrapped it around her hand, like a make-shift glove, and picked up the handle of the iron, returning to the table piled with linen napkins.

Silversmith said, "Well, I have heard of Benjamin Franklin. He's the ambassador to England."

The housekeeper took some of the un-ironed linens and laid them on the table before her. She dipped her free hand into a bucket of water sitting nearby, and sprinkled the linen napkin with water from her fingers. Then she ironed it and handed it to Silversmith to fold.

The housekeeper responded to Silversmith with, "Indeed, he is. Benjamin Franklin took one of Miss Wright's dyed silk bolts over to Queen Charlotte as a gift. A diplomatic gift. Something about showing the Queen how the Colonies can make quality goods."

"So Susanna Wright is a silk worm farmer or some type of fabric weaver?" Silversmith queried as she folded the napkins.

The housekeeper was quickly flicking water on the squares of cloth, swiping each one with the heat of the iron and pushing it to Silversmith, then grabbing the next one. Silversmith tried to keep up with the pace.

"Miss Wright was first in her Pennsylvania colony to export silks. She has never married because, as a Quaker, she felt once she married, she would have to be subservient to men. But as a single business woman, she could conduct business as an equal with the men. She could conduct business with them and they would respect her as an equal."

"So the two friends of Benjamin Franklin, the older ladies, Elizabeth Timothy, the newspaper publisher and Susanna Wright, the Quaker silk farmer, will be in this Meeting town instead of coming here to the estate of Lady Sarah Wilson?" Silversmith clarified.

"Well, Elizabeth Timothy might have died, but one of her seven children should be around. She wrote some books, you see... so the children stock them in the bookstores in town."

"Oh, speaking of selling things in town," Silversmith rose from the table, having folded the last napkin, "I have been instructed to purchase some items in town and I believe the carriage is waiting outside. Is there anything else I could help with before I run the errands, then come back and unpack?"

"Nay. Be off with you to run your errand. If you help in the household, then you are welcomed to stay for the season...was it Silversmith?" The housekeeper asked.

Silversmith smiled and turned to leave through the kitchen door. The carriage was waiting for her. Billy Dawes sitting on top with reins in hand. Jane had stepped out onto the gravel driveway.

"Oh, there is my mistress, now," Silversmith said, "Thank you so much," She said to the housekeeper.

The housekeeper went to a chalkboard on the wall and looked at the names. Her finger stopped at Hargreaves.

"Oi!" the housekeeper shouted at Silversmith, who turned around just outside the kitchen door. The housekeeper bustled after her.

"Mistress?" the housekeeper challenged, "my board says Master Hargreaves." The housekeeper looked skeptically at Silversmith. "The invitation was sent and accepted by a Mister...not a Miss. Not a Missus. Not a Dame..." She put her hands on her hips and approached Silversmith, "What goes on, here? We demand honesty and integrity in this household. Explain yourself."

"Yes. Well..." Silversmith haltingly started, awkwardly looking at her Mistress Jane. "Mistress Jane is here representing her Uncle Floyd, so really the only adjustment to make is to note that Miss Jane will NOT be able to address the loneliness of Lady Sarah

Wilson quite the way Lady Wilson may have originally uh...anticipated." She laughed nervously while thinking of what else to say to calm the territorial housekeeper.

Silversmith added, "If I may take the liberty, I find you very knowledgeable and feel I would learn so much from you during my stay. I... I think Miss Hargreaves will find...the company of the other guests...also...invigorating."

With that the housekeeper relaxed and said, "Aye. Always good to be around folk who share your values. Tend to your mistress, then... I just think Lady Sarah Wilson would have preferred a Floyd over a Jane..."

The housekeeper shrugged, again, walked back into the kitchen to correct the names on the chalk board. Another kitchen staff member closed the door behind the housekeeper.

Silversmith walked quickly to the carriage.

3 CHAPTER 37: (APRIL 1776) Bryce and Witherspoon Identify Possibilities

Inside the Hargreaves residence, all, including the Hargreaves' butler, Witherspoon, and Bryce Aiden Tyler, the business partner of the deceased, continued their informal investigation of Floyd Hargreaves' death. They were doubtful that it had been "self-murder", as Magistrate Pinkney was too quick to assess. None, however, were able to ascertain how it could have been executed, if it were murder.

The men struggled in their efforts to create a plausible explanation, satisfactory enough to gain the attention of Magistrate Karl Pinkney to open a formal investigation and capture the culprit.

Mr. Tyler paced as he and the Hargreaves' butler discussed possibilities of how this unfortunate circumstance could have been performed by one of devious intentions.

"If the shot came from where those standing outside heard the shot, then how could it have hit Mr. Hargreaves if he was over there?" Bryce took two strides and stopped as he a bit his lip and thought, "The angle is incorrect."

"Sir, may I be so bold as to inquire..." Witherspoon started while clearing his throat.

Bryce replied, "If you are to help me unravel this mystery, then I invite you to actively participate in this conversation. Witherspoon, I am eager to find who –not which tribal spirit- purposed to enact this foul deed. Ask."

"Sir, what, if I may, inquire ...what was the nature of the argument you had with

Mr. Hargreaves?"

"Ah yes," Bryce replied. "Well, this is highly irregular for me to share with you prior to speaking with Miss Hargreaves, but she is away indefinitely. Yes. Well. How shall I sum it up? I believe I require your assistance and perhaps if you knew the truth it would warrant your trust in me."

Bryce cleared his throat, "To begin... Floyd Hargreaves, my business partner, was approached by a man... an Indian fellow... fluent in English. Rather fluent. He said he knew there were businesses in the colonies who would hire some Indians to take people and enslave them. He wanted to know if we were one of those businesses. His concern was that middling trades folk, such as we, were portraying the natives in a manner such as to encourage fear amongst the colonists. He felt the reputation of all tribes was being besmirched."

"Sir, I still do not understand why such a conversation would cause a disagreement between you and Mr. Hargreaves..." Witherspoon commented.

Bryce replied ashamed, "Mr. Hargreaves wanted to dedicate our resources to help fight such a scheme. I felt it was pointless... a waste. We barely had enough staff to handle our businesses as it was... and this Indian affair was no concern of ours. We neither promote nor sell slaves, so why waste time on it? Mr. Hargreaves, however, felt that if we did not actively stop those organizing this endeavor, that it would eventually harm our business. He said it was my God given duty to ferret out the malfeasants and hand them over to those in charge... to Magistrate Pinkney, as it were."

"And do you think the Magistrate would have dedicated his men to that investigation?" Witherspoon asked.

"In my considered opinion," Bryce started, "if Magistrate Pinkney believes investigating Floyd Hargreaves's death is pointless, he would not care about some educated Indian fellow who holds that the reputation of all tribes are being tainted by such activities." Bryce sighed, "I wanted to concentrate on our business and let the slave traders attend to theirs. Mr. Hargreaves disagreed and felt that profit could be made if all businesses of all industry agreed to not use slave labor. This is why we argued."

"Do you, sir, employ slaves?" Witherspoon asked.

"Oh, everybody has slaves," Bryce defended. "Well, no more than necessary. I mean in my household... They are not as skilled as you are, Witherspoon. You could replace ten of them." Bryce looked down at the ground. "Yes. I see Mr. Hargreaves' point, now. How productive is it really when your staff is forced to do a task?" Bryce concluded.

Witherspoon replied, "I have always been paid well for my work. Mr. Hargreaves provided education when needed. Some in my profession seek out apprenticeships to pass on skills to the next generation." Witherspoon continued, "I doubt slaves are given such consideration."

Bryce pleaded, "I wish you would not take Mr. Hargreaves side on this one, Witherspoon. You see if some businesses employ slaves, they offer their product for far cheaper and how can we compete with that?"

"By making a better product, Sir," Witherspoon replied. "Product manufactured by unwilling hands and the hearts of resentful saboteurs will always be inferior to those made by willing skilled workers."

"I see your point, now, Witherspoon," Bryce sighed. "If it were an inconsequential matter as I had originally thought, then... then... my business partner might not have been killed...."

"When I served as footman in another household, sir," Witherspoon shared as he adjusted his shirt cuff, "I was loaned to help at a soirée of Widow Degraffenreidt and Widow Stagg."

"How long ago?" Bryce asked, curious.

"Some thirty years ago," Witherspoon continued. "During these and other events hosted by these women, they would give away slaves as door prizes."

"Really!" Bryce replied, astounded. Bryce Aiden Tyler suddenly composed himself, stood upright and straightened his waistcoat, checked his pocket watch, and strode out into the hallway. "Well, Witherspoon. I doubt today people would treat other people with such disdain... even if they are slaves."

You know, I simply do not trust this strange medicine man you speak of. He could have been a charlatan and Mr. Hargreaves could have been in a gullible mood."

"But he must have found something of consequence, sir," Witherspoon commented. "Otherwise, why kill Mr.

Hargreaves?"

"Indeed," Bryce started thoughtfully. "Then, let us try to discern the manner in which one might get a body across the room without making footprints in the dust..." Bryce slumped his shoulders, now realizing the gravity of his loss.

Witherspoon said, "The clock, sir."

"The clock?" Bryce Aiden Tyler asked.

"The town clock, Sir." Witherspoon explained, "It struck the hour as you knocked that day, but then it struck once more. However, I recall that the second gong was not an echo, nor did it sound like the town clock... it was different..."

"Do you think it could have been a firearm rapport?" Bryce asked trying to remember.

"Sir, all that I recall is that it echoed. It was a loud sound, never the less" Witherspoon replied. "I believe I must seek out Mr. Tweedbottom." Bryce stated as he headed to the front door. "Sir?" Witherspoon asked as he opened the door for Mr. Tyler.

"Yes?" Bryce asked as he put on his gloves.

Witherspoon replied, "I know slaves are collected from all lands, such as Bight in the region of Biafra, which is very active in slave trade. And during a sea voyage, I have heard half become diseased, and a significant amount actually die in transport."

"Slavery is not my trade, Witherspoon," Bryce replied, quietly.

"But, sir," Witherspoon added, "What if this medicine man who spoke with Mr. Hargreaves was correct... what if it becomes easy for slave traders to capture actual colonists and force them into slavery? Slaves captured right here would not die during transport because they are already here. Perhaps that is what Mr. Hargreaves was trying to prevent. Perhaps he was working out of avuncular protective instinct once his niece Jane had arrived. Perhaps he feared she might be taken and was trying to make this colony safe for her."

Bryce popped his hat on and gave it a tap as he stepped through the front door, saying, "I don't think the slave traders are willing to kidnap their own neighbors as a fresh source of inventory for slavery. I believe those who have endured the ocean voyage to settle in a colony here will not contribute to the theft of their loved ones just so the crown could make a profit. "

"I suppose it would depend on how lucrative the offer was and how flexible ones morals are. It is always easiest to do nothing when evil schemes bud..." Witherspoon gave a short bow as he started to close the door behind Bryce Aiden Tyler.

Mr. Tyler turned around and faced Witherspoon as he put his hand on the door to stop it from closing. He said,

"Witherspoon. Earlier, Mr. Tweedbottom implied to Miss Hargreaves that I was involved somehow in her uncle's demise. I notice you possess sound insight. I would like to stroll to Mr. Tweedbottom's shop. Are you able to accompany me?"

Witherspoon looked at Bryce Aiden Tyler before he replied with, "Will you engage Mr. Tweedbottom for the purposes of righting your reputation with Miss Hargreaves? Or to confirm Mr. Hargreaves died by his own hand? Or do you believe Mr. Tweedbottom may have some knowledge of who might have murdered Mr. Hargreaves?"

Bryce replied with a smile, "As a gentleman's gentleman, I would charge you with the responsibility to ensure that this gentleman," Bryce pointed to himself as he continued, "does not meet the same end as your previous gentleman." He took a deep breath and then added, "Why don't you accompany me and thereby discover what I shall discuss with Mr. Tweedbottom?"

4 CHAPTER 38: (MARCH 1776)
Arriving at Dunlap's

The dusty carriage made its short ride from the Sarah Wilson estate and rolled up to the front of the Dunlap home.

This home was neatly nestled in the countryside just a short carriage ride from the village where the print shop was located, and a full day's journey from Meeting Town.

Billy Dawes hopped off his perch and opened the carriage door to welcome his three passengers: Jane, Polly and Silversmith.

"Here is the Dunlap residence," Billy said as he opened the carriage door.

"Marvelous, I'll simply ask the lady of the house if she can take this poor creature in," Jane held out her hand to have Mr. Dunlap help her out.

"Well," Billy replied, "Pardon me saying so, but the Dunlap's are middling folk. They'd tell her to head three towns down to an inn if you were to do that. And inns require coin for payment... not pig."

Silversmith added, "What if the inns are filled? Oh, and Miss Jane, Mrs. Mulhoolin, here is with child so may need to have a woman around to tend to her... Not sure an inn is the proper environment..."

"What do you suggest, Mr. Dawes?" Jane asked withdrawing her hand.

Billy replied, "Let me introduce her slow like, Miss Jane. Through the servants. Explain a bit, you see. Have them ask the mistress of the house..."

Jane acquiesced, "Very well, Mr. Dawes. These are people you've delivered for in the past, so you know how they work." She turned to Silversmith and remembered to say, "Oh, and Silversmith..."

"Yes, Miss Jane?" Silversmith replied.

Jane reached for her carpet bag still under the seat and said, "I almost forgot. Polly, has entrusted us with some vellum. Perhaps while here, you can ask the staff if they have some of that powder paper they sprinkle on the vellum to drink in the ink." Jane pulled out her carpet bag and extracted the crumpled vellum from the pocket.

Polly turned to Silversmith, "I'd so appreciate it being restored. I don't want to impose on these Dunlap folk to do more than just take me in, and but I truly don't want to replace that paper."

Billy suggested, "The Dunlaps print on regular wood pulp paper. They make large quantities of notices and such for me to deliver to some of the other towns. I've not seen them ever use Vellum. I don't think it's the stuff for a printing press. More like calligraphy done by hand," Billy paused, then continued with, "The Dunlap printers may not have that powder stuff lying about in their home, but there is another shop in town I can take you to get supplies for that sort of thing. I can ask Mr. Dunlap for advice."

"Well," Silversmith interjected, "I've not tried to restore vellum, but if it's just crinkled a bit, perhaps I could press out the wrinkles, maybe dip it in starch to stiffen it and give it a go when I'm pressing Miss Jane's dresses."

"I wouldn't do that, Silversmith," Billy Dawes mentioned. "Vellum is calf skin. You have to melt creases out by steaming it lightly. Maybe rub pure alcohol on bits, then re-stretch it until it dries."

"Oh," Jane replied, "I didn't realize it was so involved. Mr. Dawes can you restore it?"

Billy replied, "I'll be sleeping in the stables with the horses, so I don't think I'll have the expertise nor the supplies to, Miss."

"Oh, no..." Polly looked down at her folded hands. It appeared she was about to cry. "It was the last thing her husband gave her before..." Jane whispered to Billy Dawes.

Silversmith put an arm around Polly, "Cheer up, Mrs. Mulhoolin. We'll figure it out." "Oh, Silversmith, please call me Polly," Polly softly added, "Everyone here, please... call me Polly".

Jane looked at Polly, Silversmith and then Billy Dawes. She said, "Right. I will wait in the carriage. Mr. Dawes, kindly introduce Polly in the manner you deem fit. Get her situated with the Dunlap staff here. Then, Mr. Dawes, you could drop me off at Lady Sarah Wilson's estate. I'll remain in my chamber at the estate while Silversmith goes into town with you to pick up some items for me, as well as escort Polly's vellum to whomever can fix it." She turned to Polly and added, "Would that be an acceptable plan?"

"Thank you," Polly said, "I appreciate it."

"The Dunlaps," Billy helpfully interjected, "Are plain middling folk. No lords. No ladies. No titles, here. Just basic household staff. Cooks, maid, gardener. And the Butler's name is Simms."

"Quite." Jane thought of her own transition from full staff to just a butler and maid and said, "Just the basic staff."

Billy paused, "Silversmith might get on better with Cook and since you've been getting to know Polly in the carriage, you can tell Cook what you think of Polly."

Silversmith nodded.

Jane interjected, "Silversmith, after you and Mr. Dawes get Polly placed, will you go with Mr. Dawes into town? If we are to remain here for a while, you may need to become acquainted with the shop owners for future errands and such."

"I will be happy to do that, if Billy... Oh, I mean Mr. Dawes... would be kind enough to drive me. I expect if we stay the season at the Wilson estate, Mr. Dawes would drive me into town frequently..." Silversmith glanced at Billy, who couldn't help but nod in the affirmative in return.

"Yes, you can call me Billy," and slowly turned away blushing gruffly.

It took some time as Billy Dawes, bashful carriage horseman, ran around to the back servant's entrance and knocked.

Once the door opened he was heartily greeted and invited inside. The staff not only knew him, they welcomed him.

Billy Dawes asked, "Is the master

home?" He looked back at the carriage and indicated with a wave that he'd be inside and for those awaiting to expect a signal to time their introduction.

The Dunlap's butler, Simms, sitting at the long servants table polishing silver, said, "Soon, Mr. Dawes. He is in town at the print shop."

"Oh, regular every day print jobs, eh?" Billy Dawes prodded.

Butler Simms replied, "He's been having meetings with people about if some such thing should be printed in English, in German or both. Apparently, it's a large order and causing Mr. Dunlap a great deal of consternation. I've been trying to buffer him from the usual things which often interrupt his routine."

"Ah, the master doesn't want anything disrupting his routine, eh? And how is Mrs. Dunlap?" Billy asked. Simms replied, "The lady of the house stays in the house."

"Oh, would she like a companion to while the hours away as Mr. Dunlap busies himself in his print shop in town?" Billy asked.

Simms got up from the table and, now curious, walked to Billy.

"We found a lady in distress. Well mannered, but she needs a place to stay until... Her husband's gone missing you see. Have you a spare room for her?" Billy asked Simms.

"We do have one room currently not occupied," Simms said, "But to take her in, a stranger, I'd have to ask Mrs. Dunlap for permission."

"Oh, we brought payment, but not in coin, you see..." Billy shared. He stepped outside and brought in one sac and placed it on the chopping table.

Cook walked to it. "Its fresh boar meat?" Cook asked.

"Aye. We've got about three hundred

pounds of it... and the lady whose family has hired me as coachman for the season also employs a maid, named Silversmith. She can show you some new ways to prepare it. Can I fetch her, as well? Silversmith?"

Cook replied, "By all means..."

Billy ran outside and signaled Silversmith to come inside.

After Silversmith shared with the cook how to prepare the boar meat, Simms, the Dunlap butler concluded that the meat might indeed be presented to Mrs. Elizabeth Dunlap as payment for lodgings.

"If you are to ask the Mistress, Simms," the Cook shared quietly with the butler while placing a platter in his hand, "Then take her some samples of the meat cooked the way Silversmith just done showed us... I've broken it up into bite-sized morsels of this, um... this..."

"Bacoun," Silversmith softly interjected.

"Yes. Bacoun," Cook nodded a thanks to Silversmith, then turned back to the Dunlap butler, Simms. "And take this small cup of apple cider and ask if she would accept the boar meat as payment for Mr. Dawes' friend as she needs a place to stay for a while. Explain she is with child..."

"Ah," Simms noticed examining the tray he held, "This is missing a fresh bloom from the garden. I shall return."

With a deft pivot, the Dunlap butler, Simms, turned on his heels and went in search of the perfect flower to adorn the bacoun and apple cider ensemble, which Cook had arranged on a tray.

Assuming Mrs. Dunlap would accept, Cook asked the head housekeeper to instruct the maids to remove the clutter from a large closet. They would convert it into a private room for this new guest.

The Dunlap Cook, looked at Silversmith and then out the window at the carriage, "You've got somebody still in that carriage," the woman said to Silversmith.

Billy Dawes turned to Silversmith and said, "Since you've been talking with the Polly woman inside the carriage, could you share what you know with Cook? She is a great judge of character. Give a signal when Polly should come in. I'll be outside minding the horses and being at the ready should Miss Jane need anything."

Silversmith nodded.

5 CHAPTER 39: (MARCH 1776) Polly Waiting in the Dunlap Carriage

After the Dunlap cook pointed out the window, asking who was waiting in the carriage, Billy Dawes went outside to mind the horses and let Polly know that Silversmith would give a signal when it was time for Polly to introduce herself.

Billy knew that the servants had to like Polly before they could convince the Mistress to take in a boarder.

Silversmith responded to Cook's comment. "Yes. That's Polly out there." Silversmith commented, "My mistress, Miss Jane Hargreaves, is in the carriage, waiting. If you like Polly, then we can introduce Miss Jane to your mistress."

"Do all of you need lodging here?" the cook asked, looking over the boar meat.

"My mistress and I will stay at the Wilson estate for the season," Silversmith explained. "So, only this Polly seeks lodging?" The cook asked.

"Only Polly requires lodging," Silversmith affirmed. "Do you know anything about her?" Cook asked.

As Cook and Silversmith spoke, Simms, the Dunlap butler, had quietly returned with roses from the garden. He went to a cabinet and selected a small vase. Then, he went to the sink, where he picked up a knife and stripped the stem of thorns and leaves.

"This will make the presentation of the tray of bacoun complete," Simms muttered to himself. He moved the mug of apple cider over to the edge of the tray to make room for the vase, but some other adjustments had to be made before he was satisfied with this presentation of Polly's lodging payment to Mrs. Dunlap, mistress of the household.

"The woman," Silversmith shared with Cook loud enough so Simms could overhear, "is Polly Mulhoolin, that is, just shared something about settling the lands of Benjamin Burden on the carriage ride over here." Silversmith shrugged, "Every moment I learn something new about her."

"Oh, you mean Benjamin Franklin?" Cook asked.

"No. Well," Silversmith thought a moment, "I do believe she said it was a Mr. Burden. He is a fellow who owns or owned land in the Virginia Colonies. He needed to populate his property, so he offered free land to anybody who would build a home. Polly told me other colonies besides Virginia offered such headrights. Georgia, where her husband has land, North and South Carolina and... Maryland, where Lady Sarah Wilson lives. At least that is what Polly said. You see, her passage was paid by a respected family. It was a name which sounded like a bell, but that is not important. The point is, she served her indentured term, fulfilled her contract, and is a free woman. But we found her on the side of the road. She explained that she and her husband had been attacked, so need a place to recover. She may also need to find her husband. You really will like her."

"Attacked?"

"Yes," Silversmith shared, "but not somebody who would have followed her or would bring harm to this household. By Indians. You can tell Polly was raised to be well mannered. She and her husband built their home - the one that was attacked - the one she feels she cannot go back to - in the wilderness. It is why, I suspect, she has plans to...one day in the future... to build again."

"So," Cook said thoughtfully, "now that she is free, she wants to build a cabin in the Virginia Colonies? I mean she doesn't want to build a hut for garden tools, does she?" Cook asked.

"Well, she strikes me as intelligent, and I think she mentioned she wanted to build a few structures so she can rebuild here what was lost in Ireland." Silversmith added, "She's with child, so she is wanting something for her children to live in."

"A baby?" The cook exclaimed.

"Well, it appears so," Silversmith explained. "This is why she is not able to travel much. She would vacate these quarters as soon as the baby arrives, but she has already lost her husband in this tragedy. Surely you can take pity on her and help her keep her own child..." Silversmith paused then added, "Mr. Dawes said you were a kind and compassionate household, and that is why he feels loyalty to Mr. Dunlap and wishes to do whatever printing deliveries your employers need to keep them in business... and to pay your salary... Living in any new colony is not easy, is it?"

Silversmith looked at Cook and Simms.

They both looked away. "Surely," Cook replied, "so... the land. The land your Polly wants to..." Silversmith encouraged Cook to finish her thought with, "Yes?"

Simms interrupted with a question, "How long has this fellow been giving Virginia land away?" The butler Simms was delaying his departure by carefully arranging the leaves and smaller wild flowers and roses in the vase.

Silversmith turned toward Simms, the butler, and said, "I don't rightly know. It was a grant called Burden's grant, if I recall..."

"One benefit," Simms replied, "...of working in the home of printers is that we have several reference guides all over this house. Let me see, now..." The butler left his tray and went to a cabinet, opened the door, and looked at several book spines, running his finger across them all.

"Our butler," Cook laughed, "...is very thorough indeed. I agree with Simms. We should find out as much as we can about her before even asking our mistress if she can stay with us."

"I found it," Butler announced as he opened a book and ran his finger along some words on the page. "What is the summary of this Burden's Grant, then? Is it legitimate? In Virginia?" Cook asked.

The butler, Simms, walked closer to the window to catch a beam of light to aid in his reading. He replied, "Burden's Grant was from 1737. He owned 100,000 acres and was given ten years to settle one hundred families. If he did not, then he would lose his lands. It says he was successful and recruited all one hundred families by 1739."

The cook asked, "Anybody we know?"

"I can list the names," Butler commented, while still looking at the book. "The Prestons, Paxton, Lyles, Stuarts, Grigsby, Alexander, Crawford, Cumminse, Brown, Wallace, Wilson, Carutherses, Campbell, oh and the

McCampbells as well as McClungs, McClure, Matthews, McCues, McKees and McCowns and the Moores. Are any of those family names you know?"

Silversmith said, "Those all seem to be Irish, Scottish and British family names." Cook observed, "All here in this country because of that Benjamin Burden fellow?"

"I wonder," the butler asked, "...if Polly knew of somebody in the Shenandoah county of the Virginia Colony. It says here that it was formed in 1772 and had about twenty thousand residents."

Silversmith commented, "Polly shared that if she cleared an acre of land in the forest, she could amass about thirty cords of wood. I think that's about sixty or seventy trees. That would be enough fuel for the hearth and clear the land for her to build a cabin... Said she'd store her wood off the ground so it stays dry. Apparently oak takes longer to dry out." Silversmith shrugged, "I think she has dreams to build something on the order of thirty cabins on one hundred acres each."

"Three thousand acres would definitely be a legacy for her child or children," Cook commented.

"Three thousand?" Simms exclaimed, "That's larger than the County of Shenandoah taken from Fredrick, which was about seven hundred and sixty acres. Only County Rockingham, taken from Augusta, would be larger. Your Polly's dreams are actually greater than two entire counties in Virginia?" Simms smiled at her lofty ambition.

"You have to remember, she was a lady," Silversmith emphasized, "...and she's quite anxious not to merely survive, but to rebuild her family name. She has been kind to me. I think she'll be appreciative of all the Dunlap staff, here. My mistress is in the same situation as Polly wanting to restore the fortunes lost. It's a burden I don't have, but I think she would be very honest with you if you were to ask her."

Silversmith opened the Servant's door to the kitchen, and with an arm wave, beckoned Polly to get out of the carriage and come into the kitchen.

"I can't imagine living in thirty homes," Cook shook her head.

"Oh," Silversmith continued, "I don't think she needs to live in them, just build them."

"Leaving them vacant?" Simms asked, shaking his head. "Perhaps she has not yet fully considered the details of this dream of hers..."

Simms, replaced the book on the shelf in the cabinet from whence it came. He closed the cabinet door and walked to the tray of bacoun he was to deliver to Mrs. Dunlap, mistress of the house.

"Does Polly want to take advantage of Burden's Grant? Buy land from the families already living in Virginia who settled the land as a result of Burden's grant? Or does she want to build in another forest in yet another colony with terms similar to Burden's Grant?" Cook asked.

"Well, I cannot stay to hear her answer," Simms replied as he grabbed the tray with the beautiful flowers in the vase, "I must find out what mistress thinks of this all. Please have Polly remain here until I return. I wouldn't want to shock Mrs. Dunlap, you see, but I will ask for permission to lodge this Polly women. This bacoun is delicious...."

Simms pivoted neatly and, once again, left to search for the mistress of the house with tray in hand.

Leaving Jane inside the carriage, Polly hopped out in response to the signal Silversmith gave her. She headed toward the Dunlap kitchen.

The cook looked out again and wiped her hands on her apron then walked outside beckoning Silversmith to follow, "Introduce us then... I assume that woman walking toward us is our potential lodger."

Silversmith nodded to Cook, then greeted Polly just outside the servant's entrance with, "Polly, this here is the Dunlap cook."

"Chef, mind you. Head chef." The cook corrected, "Cook is my name, you see. Or it is what they call me. Makes it easier to be named your profession, I find... although you are not a Silversmith, are you?" Cook looked closely at Silversmith.

"No," Silversmith replied. "After I was orphaned, I was taken in by a silversmith, who knew the Hargreaves. The parents of my mistress. They employed me as a servant...and the name became mine."

Silversmith turned to Polly and repeated the introduction. Polly bowed politely, "A pleasure to meet you, Cook."

"And you, Girl. What county are you from? What's your family name?" Cook asked as they all walked back into the kitchen.

"Mulhoolin, but over here some have called me Mulhollin," Polly shared.

"Is that a county Ulster name?" Cook asked. "Some of the other servants around here are from Ireland... and other places..."

"It 'tis indeed," Polly replied with a smile, glad that somebody knew of the country from whence she originated.

"You must tell me," Cook smiled at Polly. "Tell me all about your voyage over here." The cook noticed Polly's belly and asked, "Is your husband an Irishman?"

"No," Polly started, glancing at her abdomen, and thinking about her unborn child. "My husband is from England. We briefly met after I arrived on a horrendous sea voyage. You see, a family sponsored my voyage in exchange for a few years of household service. After I completed my service, I wrote a letter to my Button to let him know he could love a free woman... I had paid all my voyage debt in full."

"Sometimes the cost of coming over here can make for a romantic story, Polly," Cook smiled. "So, you and Mr. Mulhoolin are expecting a family, eh?"

"Yes. Well no..." Polly stuttered. "Yes. We will have a family soon, but Mulhoolin is my name. You see we married in haste and I did not take his name formally. I would like to rectify that once I find a man of the cloth to properly record it in a church book of records," Polly sighed to herself. "But, first, I would need to find out if my husband is still alive..."

"Let me make a cup of tea and you must tell me all about it," Cook soothed. "Mrs. Dunlap asked Mr. Dunlap to get a stove designed by Francois Cuvills", Cook smiled as she put a kettle on the hot metal top. "So we have both a hearth and a stove. I'm still getting used to it."

71

6 CHAPTER 40: (APRIL 1776) Talking with Tweedbottom

Witherspoon, the Hargreaves butler, locked the front door of the now empty residence and put the key back in his jacket pocket. He then straightened up, and accompanied Bryce Aiden Tyler out doors. It would be a long walk. They could have taken a carriage ride, but both men found it useful to discuss issues during the long stroll.

Once they got to the center of the colony where the shops were, they lingered outside Tweedbottom's tailor shop. After peeking into the window, they observed that Mr. Tweedbottom was

72

engaged in a heated conversation with his assistant.

Witherspoon was hesitant, but Bryce Aiden Tyler boldly walked in, to better overhear the angry interchange between Tweedbottom and his assistant.

Mr. Tweedbottom seethed at his clerk, "No, we are not short of funds, but they simply have not yet paid me."

The clerk replied, "I don't know how to reconcile these books, sir, since the shop lacks adequate income to offset debts. I'm not even certain all these debts were from the shop, as I don't recall them, yet here they have been written... in your hand... Perhaps if you could tell me the amount we should expect... I could..." The earnest assistant inquired.

Tweedbottom barked as he snatched up a pair of tailor's shears, "I pay you to do as I direct you to do! Before I can share my books with investors, these books must look balanced. Balance them, young man!" Tweedbottom threw the tailor shears at the clerk, who deftly ducked to narrowly avoided the shears striking him.

The tailor's assistant, trying to be humble, yet used to these tantrums, clutched the books to his chest and with quivering voice said, "Yes, sir. May I jot a reason as to why the brown butcher paper you logged was so expensive?"

"Write anything," Tweedbottom's reply made his face turn red.

"But Mr. Tweedbottom," The clerk started, "I don't recall having such paper in this shop, so I do not know it's purpose..."

"Insolence!" Tweedbottom smacked the assistant across the face, causing the heavy ledger to fall to the floor.

Then he saw Bryce. The nervous clerk gathered the book up in one hand, rubbed his face with the other, and quickly darted out of the room.

At that very moment, two Loyalist men walked into the tailor shop. Although they did not wear wigs, they did use white powder to lighten their hair. They also dusted the white powder on their faces to contrast with their red lips. Both men were dressed in the imported fabrics Tweedbottom was known to purvey at his shop.

Fabrics from the Far East, Europe, or other exotic places were more expensive and Mr. Tweedbottom passed that cost along to his customers by saying that the best always comes from a country established for hundreds of years. He discouraged his clients from using fabrics made in any of the colonies.

These two men were not soldiers, yet they each had a stripe of red along the hem of their cuff. The color served as respect for the British soldier uniforms, which were the same shade of red.

Casually engaged in conversation with each other, these men, loyal to the Crown, entered the shop just as the frantic assistant dashed out the very same door, with ledger book clutched in his hand.

Next, their eyes fell on Bryce Aiden Tyler, and the simple locally made fibers which comprised his waistcoat. After regarding the local clothing of Mr. Tyler, one Loyalist man turned to his companion with a look of amused distain. The other man snorted in disgust over the audacity of Mr. Tyler entering Mr. Tweedbottom's Tailor shop in such unfashionable garb.

Then, they saw the state of Mr. Tweedbottom and without a word, both unanimously decided to quietly turn about face and leave the tailor shop immediately.

Realizing his customer base was dwindling and he did need money, Mr. Tweedbottom quickly followed the men, opening the door which had just closed behind them and shouted down the street after their retreating forms, "I am open, Sirs. Please do see the new fabrics

I have for you..."

Yet, the men acted as if they did not hear Mr. Tweedbottom, so he stepped back inside the shop and turned his attention to Mr. Bryce Aiden Tyler, totally ignoring Witherspoon.

Mr. Tweedbottom asked, "Mr. Tyler, what new suit may I craft for you?"

Thinking about how to approach Mr. Tweedbottom, Mr. Tyler started with, "I am, Mr. Tweedbottom, quite aware of your keen eye for style and..." Bryce walked to a bolt of fabric and felt it, "...and your eye for importing luxury goods. Is this from England? I don't think I've seen anything so finely woven here in the Colonies..." Bryce smiled, knowing he actually had seen numerous comparable fabric samples woven locally.

"Indeed not Mr. Tyler," Mr. Tweedbottom replied, "This material is quite costly, but it would make a fine waistcoat."

Mr. Tweedbottom had now adopted such a calm façade that if one hadn't witnessed the most recent outbursts, one would doubt they had ever happened. Mr. Tweedbottom actually smiled and became quite agreeable.

Mr. Tweedbottom added, as he walked to a bolt of red fabric, "I have heard that adding red to one's cuff is what men of substance are donning these days. A fashion, I must confess, I started. You no longer need to read news from Paris and Milano, as I myself am now the sole voice of appropriate fashion for both gentlemen and ladies."

"I see," Bryce replied while closely examining the red bolt of fabric Mr. Tweedbottom was now showing him. "Hmmm. Stunning, actually. You have an eye for quality, Mr. Tweedbottom. However for myself, I would hate to have others think me rising above my station. Would you have fabric in... perhaps... a dark blue? Maybe lined with white flannel? To serve as a tailored jacket? Or even a greatcoat..."

"Do you want to look like a common sailor, Mr. Tyler? Shall I make you buckskin breeches, as well? Perhaps you'd like to ask the cobbler to replace the bows on gentleman's shoes with common leather strings." Mr. Tweedbottom laughed, "How dreary. Why not some red to show loyalty to your king?" Then, Mr. Tweedbottom protested, "The dye of indigo plants, the color to make blue, is not attractive."

Mr. Tweedbottom shook his head as he noticed the tailor shears, which he had thrown at his assistant earlier, were still on the ground. Mr. Tweedbottom reached over to pick them up.

"I'm not certain bright colors in a waistcoat would suit me, Mr. Tweedbottom," Bryce replied.

"Don't be absurd!" Tweedbottom walked quickly to his desk and found a sheet of paper to immediately start sketching one design for a waistcoat. "One aught not be afraid of being bold." He added, "I myself have packed a red velvet coat as part of my wardrobe."

"Pack?" Bryce asked casually. "Where is your destination?"

"Destination?" Mr. Tweedbottom looked at Bryce Aiden Tyler and blinked three times, then he said quickly, "I don't recall. I didn't arrange for the coach last time I went. I fell asleep in the carriage. I don't arrange these things, you know."

Such a reply alerted the keen senses of Witherspoon, who had been silent and motionless during this entire interchange. He cleared his throat and looked at Mr. Tyler.

Bryce replied, "Oh, I must be keeping you. I can place my order once you return from your... is it a holiday or business trip?" Bryce Aiden Tyler took two steps and stood next to Witherspoon, then added, "Witherspoon, let us leave Mr. Tweedbottom in peace as he must prepare for his journey."

Mr. Tweedbottom muttered to himself,

"Not everyone appreciates opera…"

Bryce Aiden Tyler walked to the desk at which Mr. Tweedbottom was sitting and dropped coins in front of him, "I would like to order the waistcoat, but have not yet decided on the fabric. Please count this as partial payment toward my final purchase. When you return, we can take my measurements to ensure a proper fit."

Mr. Tweedbottom happily wrote a receipt and handed it to Mr. Tyler, who accepted it with a bow and then left the shop with Witherspoon.

Once safely outside, and a suffcient distance from Tweedbottom's shop, Witherspoon turned to Bryce. "Sir?" asked the perplexed butler, "Are we not going to ask Mr. Tweedbottom for assistance regarding the death of…", but before Witherspoon could finish, Bryce interrupted him.

"Witherspoon, look at what we've learned," Bryce excitedly added, "He is deeply entrenched with the sympathizers to the Crown, as evidenced by his red-cuff fashion trend. He may be engaged in secret strategy, as evidenced by the reaction of the two men who entered then left the shop. He is very likely going to plan a trip to visit the very same opera singer... that... that..."

"Henry Mossop of Ireland, Sir?" Witherspoon interjected.

"Yes. At that estate of the...um..." Bryce struggled.

"Lady Sarah Wilson's estate, Sir?" Witherspoon asked.

"Yes. Well done, Witherspoon, which is why he could remember the jacket he packed, yet could not tell me the location at which he will wear the jacket. It is because he doesn't want me to know he will be travelling to see Jane Hargreaves!" Bryce added, "And, Mr. Tweedbottom is in debt and trying to cover it up in his shop books."

"I wonder what Mr. Tweedbottom's purchase of brown butcher paper might mean?" Witherspoon asked.

Bryce replied, "I assume Mr. Tweedbottom made that entry of the brown paper and inflated the cost drastically to cover another debt. He may not be forthcoming in all his bookkeeping, which might indicate he is willing to deceive in other areas, as well." Bryce took a breath and then said, "... I do think he may know something about the death of Mr. Floyd Hargreaves, but I'm not sure how to trick him into revealing it to me..."

"I see, Sir," Witherspoon started. "Shall we return to the Hargreaves residence? Would you wish me to prepare a tea for you, Mr. Tyler? Usually around this time, I would have done so for Mr. Hargreaves, you see..."

"Witherspoon," Bryce Aiden Tyler started, "Could I impose on you to make a purchase...a purchase I dare not risk others seeing me make myself..." Bryce spoke as he pressed a coin into the palm of Witherspoon's hand.

"Sir?" Witherspoon replied.

"Here is where our paths will temporarily part. I will meet you back at the Hargreaves' home after you purchase these items..." Bryce whispered the list to Witherspoon and then summarily walked away, leaving Witherspoon on the street with a coin in his hand.

7 CHAPTER 41: (MARCH 1776) Simms Asks Mrs. Dunlap if Bacoun is Enough.

Simms' task was to inquire of the mistress if this bacoun would be sufficient rent to allow an Irish girl, Polly, shelter until her baby was born and to also explain her plight.

Would mistress Dunlap take pity on the woman or send her away? Simms knew he would have to report as many details as he could so that Mrs. Dunlap could decide if she wanted to take on a boarder or not... without even seeing her.

Polly was to remain hidden in the kitchen until Simms could return with a decision.

In the sitting-room, Mrs. Dunlap smelled an intriguing aroma before she saw Simms enter the room with a plate of bacoun. Without words, Mrs. Dunlap examined the twisted piece of meat on the plate very carefully before she poked at one of the morsels with her finger, finding it very light and brittle. It crumbled under the pressure of her touch. She picked up a broken portion and sniffed it, then she spoke to Simms.

"Simms, what is this?" Mrs. Dunlap asked perplexed.

"For eating, Mrs. Dunlap. A new morsel Cook created, awaiting your review." Simms replied. Mrs. Dunlap licked a portion into her mouth, found it salty, yet intriguingly delicious.

Simms immediately presented her with the apple cider. Mrs. Dunlap took a refreshing gulp.

"In Cook's experiments, Ma'am, we found that to prepare this bacoun for storage we needed to salt it and that may result in thirst," Simms explained.

"I'm to eat these then?" Mrs. Dunlap sought clarification, "These squares?"

"Indeed. This is what the young lady brought with her as a gift in exchange for boarding her until she can recover and discover what happened to her husband," Simms explained.

"I see..." Mrs. Dunlap looked very closely at this bacoun, examining it. Then, with eyes closed, she popped another piece into her mouth and bit down. She was not expecting the crispy nature of the morsel and expressed surprise at the sound of a crunch. Then she crunched again, and again and then took a sip of apple cider.

"This is quite extraordinary, Simms," Mrs. Dunlap exclaimed. "Oh, I think we should get the opinions of the others. I realize it is not quite time for a meal and Mr. Dunlap has been spending his days and sometimes nights at that print shop." Mrs. Dunlap thought to herself for a moment. Simms stood awaiting direction. "Oh, John works so hard! We will all be glad when his project is completed..." She sighed to herself

Mrs. Dunlap continued, "Simms, we shall accept this new guest. Is there sufficient supply of this crispy..." Mrs. Dunlap struggled for the word...

"There is sufficient bacoun to last this household approximately three months, I would estimate..." Simms continued, "It is the only form of payment the lady brings with her so she is unable to situate herself at a proper boarding house, Ma'am. Mr. Dawes was hired for the season and they found this Polly in a state of distress and brought her here. Silversmith, a friend of Mr, Dawes, showed Cook how to prepare the dish. Silversmith's Mistress already has lodging arrangements at the Wilson estate, so they are simply asking we take one boarder in."

"And what do we know of this woman? You possesses great perception of character. What can you tell me of her?" Mrs. Dunlap asked as she took another bite of the crispy pork.

"She has an Irish brogue, appears intelligent, and is with child."

"Anything else?" Mrs. Dunlap persisted.

"From the brief conversation I overheard, it seems that this Polly, as she prefers to be called, was raised with manners, but she had to leave Ireland, indenturing herself to pay for passage to the Colonies. She fulfilled her contract and is now a free woman with plans to own land."

"So, she was raised a well bred lady, but worked as a servant, and might want to redeem her family name in this unknown hostile wilderness...hmmm," Mrs. Dunlap summarized. "Oh, my. It puts all my petty complaining into perspective. That poor thing." Mrs. Dunlap shook her head.

"What shall I tell the lady, Mrs.

Dunlap?" Simms asked.

Mrs. Dunlap took a deep breath. "Do ask Cook to prepare more of this bacoun and send a boy to Mr. Dunlap at the print shop. I'm not certain he would be open to having this fried pork during morning hours, but we shall let him decide, shall we?"

Mrs. Dunlap turned to her butler Simms, "Mr. Simms do get this girl, Polly, situated. I shall tell Mr. Dunlap that our new house guest shall serve as my companion until her baby arrives." Then, as an afterthought she added, "Oh, and do let Billy Dawes and his friends stay as long as they like before they must return to the estate of Sarah Wilson." She paused, "I refuse to call that Wilson woman 'lady' anything..."

8 CHAPTER 42: (APRIL 1776) The Tyler Experiment

Bryce Aiden Tyler walked up and down in front of the Hargreaves residence, awaiting the return of the butler Witherspoon.

The Hargraves butler had been instructed to procure sundries from the general store, the very items that Mr. Tyler did not want to be seen buying.

Witherspoon hurried to the front door, fumbling for his key as he tried not to drop the multiple parcels.

"Thank you, Witherspoon." Bryce said

as he started to take the parcels from the overloaded arms of Witherspoon.

Witherspoon was finally able to unlock the door. Bryce Aiden Tyler walked in and then turned around to Witherspoon before the servant could enter.

"What time is it?" Bryce asked Witherspoon.

Witherspoon glanced up at the town clock and then turned back to Bryce, "Nearly top of the hour, sir."

"Excellent. Our experiment may begin shortly." Bryce walked into the kitchen and laid down some of the parcels.

Witherspoon entered the kitchen a moment later and began unwrapping the strings from around his purchases, placing them out on the table.

Meanwhile, Bryce decided to walk out the back door and to the library window of the Hargreaves home. He peered inside through the glass.

Witherspoon had followed Bryce outside and Witherspoon cleared his throat as he offered, "Would you like me to let you in, Sir. I do have the key."

"But your key fits the front door, does it not?" Bryce asked to clarify.

"Indeed sir, not to the side doors because these all secure with solid iron bolts, as you can see. They are latched from the inside of the home, not the outside," Witherspoon offered.

"Have you a key to this window? This library window?" Bryce asked.

"I do not think the window latches necessitate a key, Sir. They all close with metal bolts from the inside and do not require any additional sort of lock," Witherspoon answered.

"Excellent. Exactly as I had thought. I had not given this much consideration until now, but I believe we can conduct our experiment, Witherspoon."

Then, the clock struck.

Both Witherspoon and Bryce Aiden Tyler listened intently as the town clock sounded the hour.

9 CHAPTER 43: (MARCH 1776) Button and Farmer Stop Before Getting to Town

Button wondered if he had decided to get out of the cart and race the farmer with his oxen in the wooden cart, he probably would have won. Button traced the sun in the sky and after long silent moments of travelling over bumpy lands, Button was determined to break the silence with the farmer.

Button looked back to the filled water jugs they had loaded in the back of the cart, then forward to the lazy oxen slowly pulling the cart.

Button turned to the farmer driving the oxen and he said, "This trail looks fresh. The grass is bent, but not enough to have worn away your wheel marks," Button commented to the farmer.

"True," was the only reply the farmer gave.

Button looked at the horizon, then said to the farmer, "After I was taken by those savages, I prayed my wife escaped them." Button wanted to fill the silence. "We will soon have our own family, you see. I am most anxious to find my wife, again. One must evaluate the challenges one faces here in the colonies when compared to the ones one will face if they decide to return home. The crown's reach is quite long. Almost inescapable. Did you leave anything behind to become a farmer here in this land?"

Button waited, looking at the farmer as he leaned forward with elbows on his knees holding the reins loosely in his hands, swaying with the lazy pace of the oxen pulling the cart.

"No," replied the farmer.

They travelled onward for some more time. In silence.

Button attempted to strike up another conversation. "You are delivering water to a town which appears to be a great distance away."

"Time is relative," the farmer replied.

Impressed he had gotten an immediate response, Button quickly added, "I did not imagine that your fields would be so very remote." Button looked up and pointed at the glowing ball hanging in the azure blue skies, "The sun was over there when we started. Now it is here. Your animals must be tired pulling this heavy cart."

"I will stop to give them rest," the farmer drawled.

"Oh?" Button looked around, searching the horizon for buildings where such animals may find a trough of water or a barn to rest. Some sign of civilization. Button found none.

"Where," Button started, "will we be stopping? I mean, there is nature all around. Peaceful actually. One would never know the atrocities this forming land is enduring with such divine surroundings."

The farmer looked at Button, but said to the beasts hauling the cart, "Whoa." The farmer pulled back on the reins and the tired animals stopped.

Majestic clusters of trees dotted a carpet of grassy gently sloping knolls, perfect for livestock grazing. They seemed to be in the middle of nowhere.

The farmer hopped down from the cart and released the oxen to graze a bit.

Taking a long rope, attaching it to rings in their noses, the farmer tied the animals to a nearby tree with enough lead to let them roam about and graze. Nearby was a small pond of water for them to drink.

As if from nowhere, there appeared a tall very tanned man with long black hair. His bearing was stoic, expressionless, and solid. It was as if he were an unmovable monument erected there years ago.

Button blinked uncertain about what to think. The farmer did not seem alarmed. The oxen acted as if this was a regular routine.

In the cart, Button reached for the reins, only to realize they were ineffectual without the oxen connected to the cart.

Button whipped around to look at the man as if trying to decide if the fellow were an hallucination or not.

The man was tall, hair below his shoulders and black as a raven. It glistened in the late afternoon sun like whale oil. Although he was wearing the doeskin *britch* and *moccasins* of a native, he wore the shirt of a tradesman. It was as if he had donned bits from various lands forming a composite wardrobe.

Button was beside himself, but after a moment, was able to formulate his thoughts.

He turned his attention to the farmer. Button assessed the farmer's reaction when he finally noticed this silent ebony-haired statue of a man. He did not react in surprise. That was all that Button needed to see to allow a cauldron of vehemence to bubble up inside him.

Button declared to the farmer, "You betray me, sir! After I relax in your friendship... After you gain my trust.... After you revive me from certain death, you deliver me to a rival tribe for the purposes of enslaving me? Have others fallen for this... this.. this ruse of collecting water to deliver to some non-existent town? Is this how you ensnare, betray and profit from the sale of a fellow settler?"

Button jumped from the cart with the force of a striking cobra. He was unaware that the reins he had recently picked up tangled around his ankle and as he leapt out of the cart, one leg was trapped. As Button realized part of him was jumping off the bench seat, while another part of him remained tethered within the cart, he tried to catch himself.

As he attempted to regain his balance, Button struck his head on the edge of the cart, sinking to the ground, head first.

10 CHAPTER 44: (APRIL 1776) Silversmith's Cooking Lesson

Billy Dawes slowed the carriage to a halt in front of the printer's house, the Dunlap residence.

He hopped off his perch and opened the door with a grand flourish, holding out his hand to assist Silversmith to step down from the carriage.

"I could have ridden up at your side, you know," Silversmith replied with a shy smile as she took his hand and hopped out.

Billy reached in to pull out some

parcels, "And have these precious items sit on these lovely carriage seats without a chaperone?" he winked.

"I'll only be a moment," Silversmith shared.

"I'll ...I'll just wait for you out here, then," Billy replied as he stepped up to his perch and grabbed a flat boar bristle brush with a leather strap nailed on each of the narrow sides of the brush. "I'll give my beauties a good brushing. It was dusty in that town with the boutiques."

Silversmith smiled, nodded and dashed in through the kitchen. She was holding one pack delicately and the other, she gripped to her chest so she wouldn't drop it.

"Oh, hello, Silversmith," the Dunlap Cook shared as she was kneading some dough. "Are you here to deliver those to Miss Polly?"

"I am," Silversmith replied, "What are

you making, there?"

The cook paused, took both her hands out of the mixing bowl and shrugged, saying, "Mrs. Dunlap says she wants something soft to have after dinner, but she also wants some crisp biscuits to have with tea... so I'm just trying to experiment."

Silversmith paused, "If there is a flavor Mrs. Dunlap likes, you just have to modify the proportions to get the textures she wants."

The cook grabbed an assistant, and said, "Go fetch Miss Polly for Silversmith, here," The assistant ran off. The cook indicated that Polly should sit at the large wooden table where the servants sat.

"Give me an example," the cook asked Silversmith.

Silversmith laid out the packages on the clean table top and then thought a moment.

"Get two mixing bowls and I'll show you... until Polly arrives. Mr. Dawes is waiting for me outside brushing the horses." Silversmith shared.

The cook picked up two clean mixing bowls and put them on the counter in front of her. "That baby is growing so fast this past month. I think your Polly will be walking slow like." Then she looked at Silversmith, "So, what goes in here?"

"The same ingredients," Silversmith started. "Lets try some basic biscuits." Silversmith pointed to a pile of washed dishes ready to be put into the cupboard. "Take that stein so you know you have the same amount in both bowls."

The cook picked up a pewter mug.

Silversmith instructed, "Now grab two spoons. A large soup spoon and a smaller one. The ones you serve during tea."

Shaking her head,the cook also got two

spoons a large one, and smaller one and laid them out on the table.

Silversmith advised, "Now is the time to stoke your fires in the hearth. Grab that metal pot. The one with the flat bottom. Rub lard on the bottom of it to keep it from sticking. Oh, you'll need two pots with lard. You'll bake your crispy ones with a medium flame for longer and the softer ones at a higher flame to crips on the outside, but let the inside remain soft. That one will cook for a shorter time."

After the cook rubbed lard on the bottom of a large black pot, silversmith continued, "Scoop one stein of flour for each bowl," Silversmith added, "...and the spoon of salt." "The big spoon or small spoon?" The cook asked, "One is half the size of the other."

"For salt, use the small spoon," Silversmith advised, then continued with, "and break one egg into each bowl. Take the large spoon...and...did you get anything off the spice ship which arrived a few weeks ago?"

"Aye," the cook replied. "Vanilla beans, and some brown sugar, tea... from the Caribbean."

"Good," Silversmith replied, "Take a bit of brandy and grind up the vanilla bean. Get some brandy or bourbon, if you have it. Then grind up the bean and put it in the liquor. Normally, you need to let the vanilla beans soak for a couple of months so that the liquor takes on the favor of the bean. But for now, we'll just chop it up a bit... Then, take one large spoonful for each bowl. If you have rose water, you can add a splash of that for flavor."

"So, we have salt, flour, vanilla liquor, and egg... all identical amounts in both bowls," the cook reminded.

Silversmith explained, "Now here is the fun part. Take your butter and the bowl on your left. That will be the soft bowl. The one on the right will be the crispy bowl."

Cook grabbed a pot of butter, asking, "How much butter?"

Silversmith pointed, "In the soft bowl, put in as much as would fit in the palm of your hand."

Cook protested, "That's not a very precise measurement. What if I like this mix and I want one of my assistants to make it... and their hand is a different size?"

Silversmith thought, "You are right. Instead, take that large spoon and scoop out of the butter pot, about... oh," silversmith continued to evaluate, "take about seven rounded spoons for the soft bowl. And for the crispy bowl, put in about eight or nine spoons. The more butter when baking will actually fry the batter a bit, making it more crispy."

Cook obliged and added the butter to both bowls.

"Now," Silversmith started, "For the sugar. Take one heaping spoon of white sugar for the soft bowl and a bit more for the crispy bowl. Say about four or five spoons of sugar. Not heaping. The white sugar doesn't have molasses in it or honey or any of those viscous properties."

The cook obliged, once more.

"And now," Silversmith shared, "you can add the brown sugar. For the soft bowl, take your stein, which you used to measure out the flour, and fill it a little less than full."

"About two thirds or more full?" Cook clarified.

"Yes," Silversmith replied, "Up to the top of the handle. Then, for the crispy bowl you will add less. About a little less than half that stein for the crispy bowl." Silversmith continued, "You see, for the more chewy texture, you need more of the brown sugar. For the crispy texture, you need more of the white sugar."

Cook asked, "Is there anything else?"

"Well," Silversmith shared, "If you want to add some nuts, such as almonds, or bits of hard candy or even chocolate powder, you can. But now is time to bake. And if you had yeast to help it rise, you could let it sit overnight, but you can also add in an extra egg white to both." Silversmith thought, "But, come to think of it, you can do that all later, for now... I think this batch is ready for baking."

Cook mixed almonds into the bowl which was to produce the crispy treats, and she added a bit of chocolate to the bowl which was to make the softer ones."There," she said, "I can tell the difference between the two!" Cook then used the large spoon to scoop out bits of dough and put the crispy ones in one pot and the softer ones in the other pot.

"Now,"Silversmith started.

Polly was coming into the kitchen with the cook's assistant helping Polly to walk.

Silversmith completed her lesson with, "Now, you cook the crispy almond batch with more butter and more white sugar on a medium heat for about fifteen minutes. Then let it cool." She glanced at the other pot with the chocolate, and added, "These you should cook over a higher heat, but for half the time, and then let them cool. You won't want to eat these until much later."

"Appreciate the techniques," cook remarked to Silversmith, then smiled, "Ah, and how are you feeling, Miss Polly?"

Polly returned the smile to Cook as she stoked the fire for the first pot, and replied, "I am surely ready to have this child, quite soon."

"Well," Silversmith nodded, "You are looking much better than when we found you at the side of that road a month or so ago."

"Yes," Polly started, "It was a horrible experience but I never thought it would lead to becoming acquainted with such lovely souls. I am so thankful for all of your friendships and kindnesses toward me," Polly shared as she looked at both Silversmith and the Cook and even smiled at the assistant, who normally felt invisible.

Silversmith continued, "Yes. Miss Jane has been a guest at that Wilson Estate for the same time. Tonight is a dinner..."

Cook interjected, "You know that house isn't hers. Belongs to some elderly man she enchanted who abandoned the harsh life of the colonies to spend his remaining years in Europe, never to return. Don't rightly know what will happen to the property when he dies, but I doubt his relatives would permit that Sarah Wilson to stay there," Cook breathed as she pushed the black iron pot onto the fire and covered it to bake the dough inside.

"Yes," Silversmith shrugged, "I'm not sure why Lady Sarah Wilson invites those of... uh... interesting character as her guests, but tonight she is having an event hosting an Irish Opera Singer. He was to arrive earlier, but apparently he had business delays, which Lady Sarah Wilson was rather vague about."

"Doesn't surprise me. Lady Sarah is vague about everything," Cook snorted.

"At any rate, my dear," Silversmith turned her attention back to Polly, "When Mr. Dawes drove me into town for my errands, I was able to pick up some nice fabric you can sew into a dress which will give you more room to grow..."

Silversmith handed the bundle to Polly, who said, "Oh my, thank you, Silversmith. I suspect I have about three months left, but feel I am already outgrowing what Mrs. Dunlap has loaned to me. And I am not in any state to be seen in public at the boutiques myself. Thank you so very, very much."

"And one more thing," Silversmith added as she handed the delicate package over to Polly. "Yes?" Polly asked as she accepted the gift.

"The parchment. That blank vellum, I mean. The one you were distraught about," Silversmith started, "Mr. Dawes asked Mr. Dunlap about where to fix your vellum, re-powdering it to absorb the ink, and so on... I didn't realize it was so involved."

Silversmith took a breath and continued, "Well, we found the man. He was very busy, you see, but he's just finished the repairs. See there?" Silversmith showed a little notch on the side which was there earlier, "See? It's the very same as the one your husband gave you. The man could not get all the blood off, but he did fix the tears and lightened the stains as best he could."

"Oh, this means so much to me," Polly said with tears welling up in her eyes. She gently opened the protective covering and softly touched all the faded stains of blood and fixed tears. The creases and wrinkles were gone, but she knew it truly was the reminder she had of her husband... this blank vellum.

"I've got to help Miss Jane get ready for the dinner tonight," said Silversmith as she touched the top of Polly's hand with concern.

"Yes. Thank you for the fabric and the vellum. Thank you..." Polly gently replied.

"In a few moments, I shall have some sweet biscuits ready," Cook winked at Silversmith. Then cook turned to Polly and said, "Would you like a cup of tea and a biscuit? It is guaranteed to elevate your spirits."

Polly nodded, unable to speak as she held back tears of gratitude.

Silversmith quietly left the kitchen and this time, joined Mr. Billy Dawes on the top of the carriage and rode back to Lady Sarah Wilson's estate. Billy Dawes was able to ride with the reins in one hand, freeing his other hand to rest atop Silversmith's.

11 CHAPTER 45: (APRIL 1776) Bryce Finds a Clue

In the Hargreaves kitchen, both Bryce Aiden Tyler and the Hargreaves butler, Witherspoon, were discussing the butler's most recent acquisitions from the General Store, which Mr. Tyler had asked Witherspoon to purchase.

"As you are the butler to Floyd and Jane Hargreaves, Witherspoon," Bryce started placing one jar of preserved fruit down onto the counter, "I wish to ask your opinion. What do you find odd about these items you've just purchased?"

"They wrapped my purchases in brown butcher paper, Sir..." Witherspoon started. "So I was able to carry it all home once bundled together."

Bryce looked at the parcels now laid out on the kitchen table. He tapped a tin of gunpowder, then a child's fishing toy. Next, he tapped some square sheets of paper. Then, he said, "What of these? Do you see a pattern?"

"I do not, Sir," the butler replied.

"Come, come," Bryce smiled, "You are an excellent butler with skills in organizing and managing a home..." He paused, adding, "You know I could use your skills in my household...but I digress..."

Witherspoon dryly commented, "I am flattered, Sir, but feel it best to consult with Miss Jane upon her return, as she employs both Silversmith and myself."

Bryce looked at Witherspoon, then back at the child's toy, "Yes, yes. Of course. Do what is proper in such circumstances..."

"Thank you, Sir. Now, Might I ask you to explain the pattern with these items?" Witherspoon asked. Bryce replied, "The toy is a miniature fishing pole game for a child."

"Yes, Sir. A stick with a string tied to it. That magnet at the end of the string, I assume, is to act as a lure or fishing hook of some sort?" The Butler mused.

"Yes, Witherspoon. Exactly," Bryce enthused, "And here this magnet will attract these paper fish as they have some metal sandwiched between two sides of the paper fish glued around the magnet." Bryce demonstrated by waving a magnet over the scattered paper fish on the table and having them all jump up onto the magnet.

"Yes, Sir," Witherspoon commented. "They snap quite literally to attention with great magnetism. So, these purchases, from the general store are for general use."

Bryce then turned to Witherspoon waiting for a reaction. Then he said, "Do you see? It is one possibility which could explain how Floyd Hargreaves was murdered."

"Sir? I am not following," Witherspoon confessed.

"Indeed. I'll explain," Bryce started. "The magnet. On a string. The paper. The gun powder... These are all tools used in the trickery of magic. The townsfolk cannot possibly believe the ridiculous story that an Indian Spirit was angry at Floyd Hargreaves for attempting to understand those natives. I mean, if the Indian spirits caused his death, why did those same spirits invite him to an opera which he loathed?"

"Perhaps the Indian spirits did not know Mr. Hargreaves very well, Sir," Witherspoon shared. "Which means, it was no spirit at all. Trickery, yes. Mystical spirits, no." Bryce firmly stated.

"Witherspoon, we must recreate the incident using our wits to try and reverse this trick which caused the death of Floyd Hargreaves."

Bryce extracted from his pocket a paper on which were drawn crude directions. He laid it out flat on the table, then looked at Witherspoon to make sure he was watching. Bryce then picked up one of the spare pieces of paper and started to fold it as the crude diagram depicted.

"I consulted a book I had, and copied these instructions earlier," Bryce explained as he continued to fold.

"It appears you are creating a folded square, Sir." Witherspoon was perplexed as he examined it when Bryce was done and handed the cube to Witherspoon. "A cube made of paper?"

Witherspoon observed and simply cleared his throat. With a flourish, Bryce Aiden Tyler announced, "Orikata". "Sir?" Witherspoon stated with raised eyebrows.

"During my business endeavors, I have received gifts. That book in which I found this diagram was one of those gifts from a fellow with whom I've conducted trade. The book explains that *Orikata* is the way the people of Japan fold paper to hold biscuits or money. Any sort of container... can be constructed from paper. There was a poem written nearly a century ago in 1680." Bryce took the cube back and blew into a corner of it inflating it until the sides of the paper became pillow like in form.

"Did the contents of this poem bear any significance to Floyd Hargreaves death? Sir?" Witherspoon asked.

"Well, the poem explained how butterflies were used during certain Shinto wedding ceremonies of the people of Japan some five or six hundred years prior. Samurai warriors would exchange good luck tokens made of folded paper strips."

"Shinto? Japanese?" Witherspoon commented, "What has a folded paper cube to do with..."

Bryce excitedly interrupted Witherspoon with, "The Japanese were not the only ones who folded paper. The Spanish Moors did, as well, calling the art 'Papiroflexia'. My point is, if two nations are aware of this art, then it is logical to assume others in this village also are aware of this art. Orikata, Papiroflexia... whatever you want to call it... the art of folding paper seems to be something that would intrigue a tailor who must constantly find new designs from other lands to create his fashions... does it not? ..."

Bryce handed the cube to Witherspoon and pointed to the hole as he continued, "Here keep this inflated by breathing into the cube."

Witherspoon took the cube and puffed into the corner.

"Feeling a bit Faint, Witherspoon?" Bryce asked concerned, "Wait there while I get my pistol." Bryce left the room and returned with weapon in hand.

Mr. Witherspoon did not know how to react, "I am feeling much better, now sir. Your weapon is no longer necessary."

"No. No. I'm not going to shoot you, Witherspoon," Bryce started, "We are going to conduct an experiment...and use that cube which you just created."

12 CHAPTER 46:(APRIL 1776) Wilson Dinner Gong -Tweedbottom & Eliza Lucas

"Silversmith walked into Jane's bedroom at Sarah Wilson's estate.

"Billy Dawes has just brought me back from the Dunlap's home," Silversmith announced as she walked through the doorway, closing it behind her. "By the way, Polly is looking very healthy."

"I'm glad you have gotten to know all the shop keepers in this place. Thank you for running those errands for Polly, " Jane replied."And Lady Sarah Wilson has been very kind allowing us to remain here for all this time."

"You were right, Miss Jane. Surprising Polly with the vellum along with the fabric for her new dress created a memorable moment."

Silversmith started with helping Jane get out of her dressing gown.

"Yes. I think she would be too embarrassed to have received it with me or her host, Mrs. Dunlap, present. It would have been awkward, but considering she spent the last few years as a servant, I felt she would be more comfortable with you. You are both Irish, after all."

"Yes, Miss Jane," Silversmith replied as she placed the garment on the bed, then went to the wardrobe to set up the gown Jane Hargreaves was to wear for later that evening.

"I've never seen somebody so upset over a blank paper such as that," Jane replied, "but I suppose if it is the last reminder of her husband... it serves as some sort of solace for Polly."

"Yes," Silversmith shared, "I spoke with Cook about recipes and also gave Polly the fabric for her new dress. She truly appreciated it."

Silversmith walked to the window and looked out onto the main pebble strewn walkway of Lady Sarah Wilson's estate.

There was not much land, not compared to other estates, but it was a large well-fashioned home nonetheless.

"Cook says," Silversmith explained, "that this place actually belongs to another man who has chosen to live in Europe never to return to the Colonies. Cook says that once he does die, Lady Sarah Wilson will be asked to leave this estate."

Silversmith glanced back at her mistress Jane, now seated at the dressing table. Silversmith inhaled the country air, then closed the large window and drew the thick Jacquard drapes across the panes of glass. The heavy woven pattern served to block out the light.

"I've tried to become friends with the guests Lady Sarah has invited," Jane shared, "but the only one I feel a true kinswomanship with is Polly. The others, I feel, would cheat me in some way, if they had the chance," Jane confessed. Then she shrugged, "But, she is allowing us to stay on for so long, I cannot complain."

"And," Silversmith added, "that opera singer fellow was delayed for his business..."

Silversmith lit a candle and placed it on a side table near the front door. Then she held up several hair ribbons next to the dress Jane would wear to dinner. Silversmith wanted to see which colors were best suited to the dress. She placed the selected ribbon down near Jane's gown and crossed the room to the dressing table.

"Oh, silversmith," Jane started, "Do leave the window open a bit for fresh air. These older homes are a bit musty." Jane scrunched up her nose.

Jane continued with, "Yes, and what business is so complex that Lady Sarah cannot explain it to us?"

"Well, I hear more men will be arriving as guests for the dinner tonight because that opera singer fellow will perform." Silversmith added, "I think he may already have arrived. I heard a bit in the servant's stair case on the way up here."

Silversmith smiled and pushed aside the drapes, opening the window just a bit.

"Tell me, Silversmith," Jane whispered, "What is your impression of the guests Lady Sarah Wilson entertains. Several have come and gone over the weeks and I feel I have not learned anything new."

"Miss Jane," Silversmith said softly as she helped smooth out Jane's hair with a boar bristle brush, "This Sarah Wilson house... or whoever really owns it... is very nice, but if you don't mind me saying so..."

"I don't mind at all, Silversmith. Go on," Jane prompted.

So Silversmith started pinning up Jane's hair and continued, "The people here... the black smith ladies, the men of business, the twin sons of the deceased counterfeiter Mrs. Butterworth, even our host, her not-quite-ladyship Wilson... Well, if I may be so bold as to say, Miss Jane, none of them seems to be the sort your uncle would socialize with. I just find it odd he would even have an invitation to come here."

"You mean because it was for an opera performance which has been delayed?" Jane asked.

Silversmith clarified, "Even if there was no opera. Just to be invited, here. I don't see anything that would appeal to your uncle Floyd for either business or social reasons."

"I am afraid that Miss or Missus Wilson, or excuse me, Lady Wilson, was anticipating my Uncle Floyd would perhaps become ensnared by her deceitful charms... Perhaps Lady Wilson was hoping for marriage... Although this place appears grand, to me it seems quite the façade. Almost like a stage production." Jane took her hair comb and scratched the marble dressing table top to reveal that it was actually painted marble and beneath that was wood. Jane looked up at Silversmith who had also observed it.

"It does seem like a stage set, indeed," Silversmith agreed, "perhaps once a lady's maid to royalty made Sarah Wilson appreciate the look of finer things, yet she cannot afford it herself no matter which man she associates with," Silversmith suggested.

Jane added, "Uncle Floyd was a good

man of business, sensible in his spending and saving. She obviously was not expecting to see me, his female niece, arrive in Uncle Floyd's stead. "

"But she did invite you to stay for the whole season, Miss Jane," Silversmith protested gently.

"Yes. And I cannot imagine why. On the surface it would seem to be a gracious overture to allow me time to grieve, but I cannot quell my suspicions. Lady Sarah Wilson's guests appear to prefer more devious pastimes." Jane observed, "Perhaps she thinks I would give her money? Oh, Silversmith, I do not know where my head has gone and why I think so ill of people so quickly these days. I know that I may give the impression that I have a fortune, however, most don't know Uncle Floyd lived a modest life because he had modest means. As you remember, I no longer have access to the extravagance I had back in London..."

"Lady Sarah Wilson doesn't know that

you trust Mr. Tyler to run the business in your absence?" Silversmith asked.

Jane started to explain, "If she were close to Uncle Floyd... as she claimed, why is it she did not know he hated opera and that Mr. Tyler was his business partner?"

Silversmith carefully continued to pin up Jane's hair, "Perhaps Mr. Tyler didn't make it into conversation... Perhaps he wasn't significant enough..."

"Hmmm," Jane mused, "I think I shall accept Lady Sarah's invitation to remain here and to grieve..." She took a deep breath, "I must indulge my irrational curiosity and find out if I'm mad or if these oddities will make sense once I piece the puzzle together."

"Perhaps Miss Jane," Silversmith started, "Our hostess... Maybe she wants you as a friend. An empty large home with fake marble tops, no matter how expertly painted, is still a large lonely house without friends... And you've been right polite to her since the minute we arrived...."

Jane smiled and stood up from her dressing table, "Yes, Silversmith, perhaps she enjoys my company... or perhaps she still hopes to ensnare Uncle Floyd's profitable labors through me... Even if it is not a huge fortune, it may be a great deal more than what she is pretending to have."

Jane walked to a marble statuette decorating a shelf and touched it, a piece fell off in her hand. Jane hastily replaced the broken bit, which again was painted wood.

Jane continued, "My uncle is too clever to have fallen for the false charms of gauche Lady Sarah Wilson." Jane looked at herself in a strip of polished metal, "Not is... was... Perhaps he was more gullible than I had thought. Perhaps that was his undoing..."

Silversmith crossed to the table by the door to pick up one of the hair ribbons she had laid there earlier.

The bedroom door flung open suddenly and Silversmith was startled to see a young woman with a panicked look.

"Oh, I'm terribly sorry. Wrong room." The blustering girl, perhaps in her early 20's blurted out in a harsh whisper, then without invitation, she entered Jane's room and closed the door behind her, leaning against the door as if to listen to whatever was in the hallway.

Jane saw the entire episode in the reflection of the polished metal and started to turn around to confront this intruder, who seemed to only notice Silversmith.

The girl spoke, "She took it from my mother, you see. My dead mother. I'm just getting it back to papa." The girl defended as she clutched something to her stomach.

Silversmith saw it was a gem-encrusted brooch. Jane turned and was about to scold this intruder.

There was a race of footsteps in the hallway rushing past Jane's room. Oddly, Jane changed her mind and she chose not to scold this intruder...this girl was obviously hiding from somebody.

The girl exhaled deliberately and then, while briefly acknowledging that Jane was also in the room with a glance, the girl shoved the brooch down her stomacher, hiding it.

"Begging your pardons," the girl said, "I'm not a thief. I'm just getting back what that reprehensible Marchionesse de Whatever stole from my papa's estate! Now, if you'll excuse me..."

The girl listened at the door to ensure the hallway was empty... Silversmith asked, "Who is the March...de...what?"

As soon as the footsteps subsided, the girl opened the door, turned to Silversmith, "I've no proof, but I doubt she's related to Queen Charlotte! I just came to collect what my father never gave her... my mama's brooch. You've been warned. Lock up your baubles ...."

Then, the girl deftly and silently stepped into the hallway, quickly closing the door behind her, scampering away down the hall.

"What did she say?" Jane demanded of Silversmith.

Silversmith opened the door and peeked out into the hallway. The girl halted, as if she was unfamiliar with the layout of the home. The girl finally selected a direction, then dashed down the main staircase before anybody noticed her.

Silversmith re-entered Jane's guest room and closed the door.

"Miss Jane, that girl is headed out the front door!" Silversmith exclaimed as she beckoned Jane to the window, where they pulled aside the drapes and looked down at the gravel strewn entrance below.

A second later, out burst the girl, quickly pursued by Lady Sarah Wilson, who was very angry, indeed. "Stop you thief!" Lady Sarah Wilson screeched in the most un-lady-like tone imaginable.

"Thief? Me?" The girl shouted in return, "Marchionesse de Waldengrave, indeed! What name are you using here? Wilson is it? A far more common name for a common thief!"

"I will not be insulted at my own home!" Sarah Wilson spat, "Eliza Lucas! Return to me what you stole!"

"Your home? I stole? This estate, only rented but six months ago... with money obtained through deceit? If I'm but a common thief, how is it you know my name, yet I do not know yours?" Eliza Lucas challenged.

"How dare you!" Sarah Wilson retorted,

"How dare I?" Eliza Lucas ran behind a

tall shrub as she continued, "How dare you dangle government positions like candy in front of the families of my Carolina Colonies! How dare you steal my mother's brooch, my only reminder of my mother! If your guests are foolish enough to believe you, I pity them, but I warn you..." Eliza Lucas burst out of the shrubbery on horseback, a horse which was previously hidden, and she turned the beast down the path.

"Eliza Lucas! I have no need for South Carolina rice! Nor your ridiculous blue dye experiments! I curse you to never marry!" Sarah Wilson screamed.

"Your curses mean nothing to me. I run three plantations when papa is away fighting for freedom of people... even people like you, ungrateful deceiver!"

By now, some of Sarah Wilson's slaves started to lazily walk outside to see the commotion.

Eliza continued, "I will teach others to grow indigo plants. These colonies will be known as the exporters of true blue!"

Eliza Lucas turned her steed and galloped straight for Sarah Wilson, stopping short of the screaming woman. Eliza leaned on her saddle as she clearly spoke to Sarah Wilson, "And I will defend my home, my colony, and this whole land from tricksters who hide behind the British crown. Do not ever return to South Carolina! Do not ever speak to anybody in my household again!"

Eliza Lucas galloped off spraying small gravel bits as she left.

The slaves of the household did not bother to pursue the young girl on horseback, despite the wildly animated urging of Sarah Wilson.

Both Silversmith and Jane were wide-eyed as they peered out their window, over hearing the entire exchange.

As Lady Sarah Wilson composed herself, she glanced up at the windows of her home and instantly both Silversmith and Jane quickly rolled to each side of the window, with backs against the wall, hoping the slightly moving drapery did not betray that they were in fact, eavesdropping.

Still with backs against the wall, Silversmith asked, "Miss Jane?" "Yes?" Jane huskily whispered, also unable to move for the moment

"I would suspect that Lady Sarah Wilson is not the sort of woman your Uncle Floyd would have befriended..." Silversmith offered.

"Indeed... and the men who use slaves as betting chips while playing cards also conflict with Uncle Floyd's values. As he said, 'It matters from whence your money comes and it must be grown, not stolen' he would tell me... I cannot imagine what would have drawn him to this place..." Jane mused.

She took a deep breath.

Deliberately, she walked back to the dressing table and slowly took a seat. Silversmith cautiously walked to the door of the room and from the small table near the door, she picked up a hair ribbon and comb and returned to where her mistress sat at the dressing table.

"So, Miss Jane," Silversmith asked, "Will you stay the season? In this house? As Lady Sarah Wilson, your hostess, has invited?

Jane sighed, "I will, Silversmith. But we are not to mention what we witnessed to the others."

"Understood, Miss Jane," Silversmith agreed. "What of Polly Mulhoolin's husband? Will we ever find out what happened to him?"

"Witherspoon found and vetted Billy Dawes, our driver. Mr. Dawes recommended the printer's house, the ..."

"The Dunlaps?" Silversmith offered.

"Yes. The Dunlaps as hosts for Polly. So she is safe to remain there during her situation. I plan to reside in this residence, the Wilson Estate."

"Why is that, Miss Jane?" Silversmith asked.

"Well, the Dunlaps do not have yet another spare room for me," Jane started and took a deep breath, then added, "I have a suspicion that somehow this stolen brooch, the raid on Polly's home, and Uncle Floyd somehow are connected... to this estate... I'm simply not sure why... or how..."

Silversmith finished with Jane's hair . Jane stood up and removed her dressing robe. Silversmith tightened Jane's corset over the cotton chemise she wore, then adjusted the ribbon around her waist to position the under-skirt. Finally, Silversmith took the cool satin and brocade gown and held it in a manner to slip it onto Jane with a rustle. Once the skirts were smoothed out, Silversmith continued to fasten up the tiny buttons, then did a last minute combing of Jane's hair.

Finally, Silversmith opened Jane's hand luggage and extracted a hand mirror for Jane to check her reflection.

Jane fiddled with her dress as she peered into the tiny mirror holding it out as far as her arm could reach. Silversmith took the mirror, stepped away and then stood still for Jane to observe herself from a distance.

Jane shared, "I'm not certain how particular these Wilson guests are. If I am to gain their confidences, I must appear to be successful. I wonder if they will notice my fashion is not current..."

"I don't think they will notice the date of your dress, Miss," Silversmith understood. "Actually, in town the shopkeeper gave me a bit of news from the London Chronicle."

"Oh?" Jane asked as she wrapped her lace shawl around her shoulders and inhaled deeply. "What does the newspaper from London say, Silversmith? Perhaps I can use the information to open up conversations..."

Silversmith took the folded paper from her skirt pocket. "Hats," Silversmith started, "are now worn upon an average six inches broad in the brim and cocked between Quaker and Kevenhuller..."

"What is that supposed to mean?" asked Jane. "That a man's hat brim should be neither loose, nor fitted to the crown? Yes, yes, go on..."

Silversmith continued reading, "Some have their hats open before like a church spout... some others wear them rather sharper, like the nose of a greyhound. . . the beaux of St. James's wear their hats under their arms, but the beaux of Moorfields all wear theirs diagonally over the left or right eye. Sailors wear their hats tucked uniformly down to the crown, and look as if they carried a triangular apple-pasty upon their heads."

Jane smiled, "Well, that's fashion for you. If we can't all get aligned about how one should wear a hat... then... we are truly in the age of anarchy."

Silversmith added, " I don't know how the other guests will wear their hair, but I do hope they like this hairstyle on you..."

Jane replied reassuringly as she looked in the hand mirror and smiled, "Oh, I love my hair. I always felt pulling the hair back, as one did in the 1760's, made one's head appear rather disproportionately pin-like in comparison to the full skirts."

"I could pile your hair on a cage like they do in the French Courts..." Silversmith offered.

"No," Jane shook her head. "I don't like the overdone high wigs... Piling hair and lace on top of head-cages. I already wear your brilliantly modified birdcage under my skirts. I do not need one on my head, as well. I do not need you to stuff extra hair or wool to cover the cage. Nor do I enjoy the smell of the greasy palmatum you smear over the cage and hair... and I always cough when you dust it all with the white powder. I also am going against fashion by eschewing the high Madame Fontange head-dresses dripping with lace, ribbons and what nots." Jane smiled, "However, I do appreciate what you've done tonight. My hair is perfect. No hat. No head cage. No white powder... and I do not need to step gingerly to keep it balanced on my head, nor be concerned about the low door frames which may bump my hair. Should there be dancing, I will be sufficiently alluring to the gentlemen with whom I shall converse this evening."

"Well, " Silversmith replied, "Madame Frontage was Louis XIV's mistress so she was in a perfect position to make other woman think that she does attract gentlemen, so they copy her." Then, Silversmith interjected, "Although, I suppose the ladies of the French court did not need to bow their heads as they always maintained erect posture during dancing... from what I've heard."

"As you know, Silversmith, I am here only to gather information." Jane spun around in her dress to show that her hair wouldn't fall off. "And if I need to make a quick escape as the dramatic Eliza Lucas did, I want to remain quite mobile. I may need to run away from a man!"

"But, Miss Jane," Silversmith said, "Maybe not all the men here are of the same station as Lady Sarah Wilson. Perhaps that Eliza Lucas should not be an indicator of Lady Sarah Wilson's character. Perhaps there will be a fellow you'll meet at dinner who would be a fine match for you... What would catch your fancy? "

Jane walked to the dresser as Silversmith handed her a pair of gloves to slip on. "Well, I want to be clear on my focus... to find out information... however..." Jane smiled and then looked up as if to recall a memory.

" I do sometimes," Jane started with a smile, "like a fellow in his white powdered wig, as long as he won't scratch his head causing the wig to slip askew. I enjoy a fragrant flower in the button-hole, and the embroidery on the daringly bright coat cuffs. Have you noticed that today men are wearing less lace, but make up for it by donning brighter eye-catching coat colors? Oh, and the way they flip their coat tails before they take a seat... hmm."

Silversmith looked down to hide her smile.

"There is nothing that gets my heart racing more than... than... a well polished shoe buckle glinting in the sunshine with gemstone accents." Jane abruptly stood up straight and checked herself. "Perhaps I've been single a bit too long."

"If that is truly the case, Miss Jane," Silversmith commented, "then if you don't mind me saying so, why have you remained simply friends with Mr.

Tweedbottom. He has come for tea. He has shiny shoe buckles... and, if I recall, when he was here at your Uncle's tragic passing, he was right there to comfort you."

"Hmm. Yes. Indeed, Silversmith. At first glance, Mr. Tweedbottom does have everything a maiden could want. Impeccable fashion sense. He owns the tailor shop in town. He has good manners at tea. He is attentive..."

"And he was there to comfort you when your uncle tragically passed away." Silversmith repeated, "I noticed he seemed very suspicious of Mr. Bryce Aiden Tyler when he arrived."

Jane took a deep breath, "Indeed. Yes. You are correct, Silversmith." She frowned.

"Well, be it Mr. Tweedbottom or a new gentleman you might meet here in this house... if you don't mind me saying, Miss Jane... I think you'd be happy with a good man..." Silversmith started to clean up and put away some items on the dressing table, as well as packing up the hand mirror safely.

"A good man, indeed, Silversmith. These knights all have dented armor, I'm afraid. All human," Jane commented as her hand reached for the door knob."

Then, Jane's guest room door opened again. A man, without looking inside, apologized for entering the wrong room, closed the door quickly and hurried away down the hall.

"Has my bedroom been placed in the center of town?" Jane, exasperated, uttered to Silversmith. Silversmith opened the door, popped her head out and closed it once more.

"'Twas Mr. Tweedbottom !" Silversmith whispered.

"Mr. Tweedbottom? Surely you are mistaken, Silversmith." Then Jane re-opened the door herself and saw the familiar form just descending the staircase.

Jane closed the door again, and asked, "Why is Mr. Tweedbottom here?"

"Perhaps he followed you, Miss Jane? He did say he liked the opera? Maybe he had his own invitation to the Wilson estate and forgot to mention it to you?" Silversmith offered.

"Either of those options is rather odd. Why did he not send a letter in advance of his arrival and inform me he was coming?" Jane mused to herself.

Then the dinner gong sounded, calling all guests to the dining hall.

"I am determined, Silversmith," Jane said with a forced smile, "to find out what on earth is afoot, here. And, Silversmith, I'm quite pleased you were such an eager student years ago when you learned to read and write... as I may need to send you on a mission of research for me. Documentation shall be required."

Silversmith offered, "Shall I also write to Witherspoon to find out what is going on back home?"

13 CHAPTER 47: (APRIL 1776)
Witherspoon's Paper Cube

In the Hargreaves kitchen, Witherspoon was reassured that Bryce had gone to retrieve his pistol only to conduct an experiment.

A moment later, Bryce was extracting his pistol from his overcoat pocket, had returned to the kitchen, and now laid the firearm on the kitchen counter.

Bryce then took a nearby candle and asked Witherspoon to light it. Once the wax got hot, Bryce took the wax and covered the hole on the paper cube to seal in the air. They waited for the wax to

153

cool.

"Witherspoon, kindly remain here while I go outside. Stand in the same place you were when you first heard the shot on the day Mr. Hargreaves died. I shall recreate the shot and I would like you to write down when you hear something." Bryce looked at his pocket watch and instructed, "I will then return and hear your report."

"My report about your rapport, Sir?" Witherspoon asked.

"Indeed, My good man," Bryce grinned as he swiped his weapon from the counter with one hand and the paper cube with his other hand. "Now do not look at me. Focus on your writing desk, as you were focused when Mr. Hargreaves died."

Witherspoon heard the front door click shut, but he did not look as per his instructions.

Outside, Mr.Tyler walked about the

perimeter of the Hargreaves home for a bit until he found a barrel half filled with water. Nearby, was a pile of hay.

Inside, Witherspoon, sat at the writing desk with feather quill nib dipped in ink, and poised to write. Witherspoon looked at the clock.

Bang.

Witherspoon heard it and quickly jotted down the time. He wrote "Shot" next to the time. A moment or two passed.

Witherspoon held his breath and then startling him, he jotted down his second note when he heard a second shot.

A few moments later, Mr.Tyler came strolling in. "Did you hear the shot?"

"Yes, Sir," the butler replied, "both of them." Witherspoon presented Bryce with the paper noting the times.

"Ah, but my good man, you have

recorded two shots and I only fired my weapon once." Bryce smiled, "But, sir," Witherspoon defended, "I distinctly heard two rapports."

"You see, the paper cube was smashed just inside the door there!" Bryce showed Witherspoon the flattened paper cube as he continued. "This is why I had to have you focused on your writing. It took me but a second to flatten it when you were not looking. If I had done it just outside the door, the sound would be slightly muffled... Is it possible, Witherspoon that the sound of the smashing of a paper cube could have been the shot you heard."

Witherspoon asked, "Then who would have smashed a cube in the foyer of the door I answered that day?"

"Hmmm," Bryce started, "Was anybody left unattended in the entrance way?"

"I generally receive the guests, and if expected, show them to the room of their hosts," Witherspoon commented, "Miss

Jane or Mr. Hargreaves. But when I heard the shot, I was the only one about. Miss Jane and Mr. Tweedbottom having tea. Silversmith in the Kitchen. Mr. Hargreaves in the library. And you were outside..."

"There must have been some distraction," Bryce said.

"I do not know, Sir." Witherspoon thoughtfully pondered, "I feel that the shot I heard was most definitely the bang caused by igniting gunpowder... I am not sure it was the flattening of a paper cube."

"I suspect," Bryce started, "The real shot was timed to be with the chiming of the town clock. So the real shot was not heard and I suspect a second sound of a shot was fired so that witnesses would confuse the time of the murder... and that could allow the murderer the ability to look innocent, when he or she is not."

"One possibility, Sir," Witherspoon stated as he thought.

Bryce smiled, "What do you think, my man? I want your opinion."

"Sir?" Witherspoon questioned, "if one possibility is that the paper cube was used to confuse the time of the murder, then what would be a second possibility?"

14 What Just Happened?

As Polly and Jane get to know more about each other and their shared common values, Silversmith, Jane's loyal lady's maid, arrives at Sarah Wilson's mansion and is getting to know the staff. Jane brings Polly to the Dunlap home and pays for Polly's lodging with the meat of the boar slain by Polly herself. Will Simms, the Dunlap butler, welcome Polly?

Meanwhile Bryce Aiden Tyler and Witherspoon identify some theories which may plausibly explain what happened to Jane's Uncle Floyd.

Tweedbottom starts to reveal his true character and what is actually motivating him. His relationships with Lady Sarah Wilson and Eliza Lucas become clear

Meanwhile, we see that Button has befriended a Farmer and has survive a harrowing experience.

The puzzle of Uncle Floyd's death is unfurling.

15 Did You Know...

In the Journals of the Continental Congress - Petition to the King; July 8, 1775

SATURDAY JULY 8, 1775

They recognized that inflamed passionate causes resulted in a clash and bloodshed, and it would not further their cause.

When a society is divided, it opens itself up for attacks from foreign powers. It causes needless loss of life. At a certain point, the infliction on fellow humans needs to stop. It is for this reason that a long letter was penned to the King. This note takes place AFTER the time period of Firebrand, but it is noteworthy to understand that the

161

people wanted peace, yet the Monarchy wanted obedience and found the Colonies to be a lucrative source of wealth.

It is this inability to value the souls who resided in the Colonies and the determination to "break them" until they quietly generated cash for the King's pleasures which is the reason why the Revolutionary War lasted from April 19, 1775 to September 3, 1783.

They asked the King to make the conflict stop. Here is one excerpt.

Knowing to what violent resentments and incurable animosities, civil discords are apt to exasperate and inflame the contending parties, we think ourselves required by indispensable obligations to Almighty God, to your Majesty, to our fellow subjects, and to ourselves, immediately to use all the means in our power, not incompatible with our safety, for stopping the further effusion of blood, and for averting the impending calamities that threaten the British Empire.

Estimates:

✓ 25,000 (some estimate a total of 50,000) American Colonists died during active service (8,000 in battle and 17,000 from disease, estimating about 12,000 of those who died from disease died as a prisoner of war on prison ships)

✓ Up to 25,000 American Colonists were maimed or permanently became handicapped during battle, but lived.

✓ 171,000 British sailors were conscripted (about half against their will) to serve the crown.

✓ 1240 British sailors killed during battle

✓ 18,500 British died from disease (mostly from scurvy, which could have been avoided if sailors were given citrus such as lemons, limes, and oranges).

✓ 4,200 British sailors deserted their posts during the war.

16 Vocabulary

In the early 1770s, before the colonies united into the United States of America, some words and terms were used, which may be explained in this section.

Marchioness - (pg 19)Marchioness de Waldegrave was one name used by Sarah Wilson.   This is a royal title of Marchioness which is in the ranks of royal peerage:
For men, King and for ladies Queen
For men, Prince and for ladies Princess
For men, Duke and for ladies, Duchess
For men, Marquess and for ladies, Marchioness
For men, Earl and for ladies Countess
For men, Viscount and for ladies Viscountess
For men, Baron and for ladies Baroness

Pliney the Elder - This is a man who was born in Como, Italy around 23 years before Christ was born. This scholar served as a naval and army commander when Emperor Vespasian ruled the Roman Empire. His full name was *Gaius Plinius Secundus.* He studied plants and developed comprehensive reference books of medicinal recipes, which some think was the seed of the pharmaceutical industry and the concept of an encyclopedia of knowledge. It is said one of his suggestions to alleviate headaches was to take pure rose petals from the Apothecary Rose, steeped in wine for a few weeks. If the mixture was warmed, it could be used as ear drops. A sleepless patient could be given a mixture of rose, mint and cloves to inhale.

Blancs- (P6) This refers to face make up used which gave the face a white color. Some say this is reminiscent of the Japanese Geisha make up. Some say it was the precursor to modern-day foundation, which today is the color of your skin. This early fashion trend was popular in Venice, Italy. It referred to *blanc de ceruse de Venise* or S*pirits of Saturn.* A recipe from 1688, "Magistry of Saturn and Lead", shows the lead face-paint was a mixture of water, vinegar and lead. The lead caused hair loss as it was absorbed through the skin and by inhalation. Cheaper, less expensive, Ceruse would substitute chalk for the more popular lead.

Headrights (p60) This was a term used in the 17th and 18th centuries to grant a pioneer a parcel of land. Frequently this was about 50 acres of land to encourage settlement in untamed regions.

Milano- (P78) This is the name of the city of Milan in Italy.

Greatcoat (p78) This is an archaic term originating from around the 1660's. It references an overcoat or a heavy coat to wear over all your other clothing.

Sitting-room- (p 86) The term "sitting" was used around 1706 to reference a time where one sits, as if being a model while your portrait is being painted. The term "sitting room" was first recorded in 1771. Today, we may call that a living room, or a room with chairs and sofas where guests may sit and chat.

Doeskin britch and moccasins -(P99) This references the leather from a doe (mature female deer) made into pants which covered a man from his waist to his knees. The moccasins were shoes worn on the feet. The term "Britch" was used in the 1620's, but by 1905 the term "Britches" was used.

ensnare, betray and profit- (P100) These were terms used to summarize the methods of slave traders. Ensnare is to capture. Betray is to gain the trust of another and then prove yourself untrustworthy, false and ready to violate all trust between two parties. "Profit", in the "slave trade", means to gain money by selling another human into a captive situation they do not want, but you force anyway because you will make money.

vague - (P112) This is a term meaning uncertain about the specifics. Middle French (around 1540) defines it as empty or vacant or wandering. The Latin term *vagas* means rambling, vacillating, or uncertain,"

Orikata or Papiroflexia- (P120) This was a term used for paper folding. Today we may reference this art of paper-folding as "origami".

Jacquard - (P127) a type of fabric which contains a woven pattern within the fabric. These were woven by hand, so became a symbol of wealth and status. One day, a weaver, Joseph Marie Jacquard, created a more efficient device which required less labor and still could create woven designs in the fabric. He created the "jacquard" with his Jacquard Mechanism system or loom.

ABOUT Wynter Sommers

Wynter Sommers is the pseudonym for an American writing team which harnesses multiple skills in technology, research, history and education. Formally trained with a PhD in Education, Wynter Sommers blends academic classroom experience, with corporate sophistication, and a passion for developing more effective student insights through engaging storytelling.

Wynter Sommers has a heart to inspire creativity and develop critical thinking skills, all to encourage readers to make wise choices in life.

Wynter Sommers takes each story and weaves the plot with classic gripping elements, which endure throughout repeated readings, revealing new meanings each time the story is explored. The small choices a reader makes in real life could have a lasting effect in future generations. This set of stories shows the origin of not just Bjorn Esterday and Sarah Paradise, but of their ancestors and the sort of world which was established, which unfolded in each generation until Bjorn and Sarah met.

It is rewarding to learn of heartfelt, thought provoking conversations taking place globally about the characters of these books. Should the reader be presented with extraordinary circumstances, it is the sincerest wish that they act with honor, truth and integrity to overcome obstacles in real life whilst the reader hones skills of self-reliance and collaborative teamwork despite barriers outside of the reader's control. Wynter Sommers hopes you enjoy the other *Bjorn Esterday Was not Born Yesterday* stories in this series.

www.ingramcontent.com/pod-product-compliance
Lightning Source LLC
Chambersburg PA
CBHW030035030726
47500CB00001B/120